THE MORNING AFTER DEATH

by NICHOLAS BLAKE

A Nigel Strangeways Mystery

"Has all the usual charm of style and characterization; I thoroughly enjoyed it."
—John Dickson Carr

Titles by Nicholas Blake available in Perennial Library

The Morning After ☞ Death

by Nicholas Blake

PERENNIAL LIBRARY ♦
Harper & Row, Publishers
New York, Cambridge, Hagerstown, Philadelphia, San Francisco
London, Mexico City, São Paulo, Sydney

A hardcover edition of this book was orginally published by Harper & Row, Publishers.

First PERENNIAL LIBRARY edition published 1980.

ISBN: 0-06-080520-X

80 81 82 83 84 10 9 8 7 6 5 4 3 2 1

To
my friends at Harvard,
with apologies for resisting
the temptation to
put them into the book

The bustle in a house
The morning after death
Is solemnest of industries
Enacted upon earth . . .

—*Emily Dickinson*

1 ☞ "We Can Wait"

"What on earth is a 'No Station'?" asked Nigel, reading a huge overhead sign as they drove into the city.

"It's a station where there are no trains, no platforms, no need to come or go," Charles Reilly said from the back. "A thoroughly un-American nonactivity."

"And no birds sing," added Sukie, trying hard to catch up.

Chester Ahlberg, who was driving, glanced at Nigel. "It's an abbreviation for North Station."

Reilly snorted. "There you go, leaking the mystery out of everything! And anyway, if that's your explanation, why don't you put a period after No? When I think of the tedious way you Americans dot every *i* in the course of your alleged conversation, yet you can't spare one little dot for the purpose of—"

"He's off again," sighed Sukie.

"*How* long have we hired you as our resident poet?" Chester's brother, Mark, asked Reilly.

"You will benefit by my presence for one whole academic year, and not a day less."

"My God!" Leaning across Sukie, Mark prodded the elderly Irish poet. "Why aren't you at Mass, anyway?"

"I was. So now I can enjoy myself. Which is more than you'd have a right to do, you guilt-ridden, transcendentalist, undenominational sons of Puritans."

1

"Will you listen to him," said Sukie. "Charles dear heart, we're here to show Mr. Strangeways the sights, not to expose him to your fey Irish prattle."

"There's no sights for the next thirty miles but eateries disguised as Nantucket whalers, pizza houses, gas stations and all-night doughnut-frying establishments. Now if only, among all these acres of advertisements, you could find one little, little touch of glamour! I don't hope for sin—that'd be asking too much, you have to have souls before you can sin, and there's no sign of them growing in this man's country."

"You Papists talk about sin as if you'd invented and patented it," protested Mark. "Over here, we take it seriously."

"*Some* of us do," his brother said. There was at this, Nigel noticed, a slight congealing of the atmosphere as when several people want to change the conversation but no one can think how to do so. On the back seat, Sukie took Mark's hand.

"I disagree," said Nigel presently.

"What?" Chester asked.

Nigel, always a compulsive reader, had just noticed, writ large on the wall of a funeral parlor, the legend

DRIVE CAREFULLY. WE CAN WAIT.

"You disagree?" asked Chester, who seemed puzzled.

"Drive carefully. We can wait," proclaimed Nigel in sinister tones. The effect ran counter to the injunction: Chester jerked the wheel and all but rammed a Cadillac which was passing them in the left-hand lane.

"Ches-*ter!*" cried Sukie.

"Sorry. What did you say?"

Nigel explained that he had quoted the undertaker's slogan.

"Well, what do you know? I never noticed that before, and I must have driven this route a hundred times." Chester's voice was light; but his knuckles were still white on the wheel. "I

guess that's pretty interesting. I get your point, Mr. Strangeways:
you were indicating that there *are* some interesting sights in this
section. Now, if you look to the right you'll catch a view of the
naval yards. And a little farther on—"

Chester Ahlberg was quite in command again, driving efficiently at the exact 50 mph limit allowed, under the bright
blue sky of the New England fall. Nigel meditated upon the
pleasure afforded by riding in another man's car, in a strange
country, all responsibilities left at home. A womb-like sensation,
highly agreeable; the more so because the womb was, as it were,
transparent, and one could see what was going on outside without having to make real contact with it. Which went for his
companions too, amicable persons in their different ways, whom
he could enjoy but need not become involved with. Chester
Ahlberg might prove a little boring; and Charles Reilly, whose
mental age—like that of most poets—seemed to oscillate wildly
between nine and ninety, certainly would be at times. But Mark
and his fiancée (but was Sukie his fiancée?) offered plenty of
entertaining variety. And yes, thought Nigel, I like them all.

"Does the grass never turn green here?" Reilly asked in his
barbed Dublin manner, gazing with distaste at the glum, brownish stuff that covered the earth, among boulders and conifers, on
either side of the highway. His companions set upon him.

This was nice too—the ready acceptance of the stranger. Of
course, Reilly had been here since the beginning of the semester
and had eased his way in. But Nigel had met the same engaging
response from the day he wrote to Ezekiel Edwardes, an old
acquaintance from undergraduate days at Oxford, now Master
of Hawthorne House, saying he wanted to do a bit of research in
the famous library of Cabot University. Ezekiel had at once invited him to occupy a spare suite in the House for as long as he
wished, had met him at the airport a week ago, and had introduced him to the resident faculty.

Chester Ahlberg, assistant senior tutor at Hawthorne, taught in the Business School; Mark on the English faculty. Their half brother, whom Nigel had not yet met, was a full professor of Classics, attached to the House but living outside. There was a strong Ahlberg connection with Hawthorne House, the father—a millionaire financier—having built and given it to the university, of which he had been an alumnus. Susannah Tate ("Sukie" to all), a graduate student at the neighboring women's college, was working for a Ph.D., the subject of her thesis being Emily Dickinson. Hence the expedition to Amherst this afternoon.

On the back seat, Mark and Sukie were wrangling amicably about the presidential election.

"Sure LBJ will sweep the country. So then what? He's a politician. He'll go just as far with desegregation as he's pushed."

"You're dead wrong. He went along with Kennedy on that, always. And he'll get further than Kennedy, because he is a politician; he can handle Congress."

"Okay, maybe he can, but do you think the South's impressed by a few blasts of hot air from Washington? Look at the way Wallace has been dragging his feet."

"Sukie wants to lead a crusade into Alabama and have another Civil War," said Chester.

"Oh, nuts. *All* I want is for state legislatures to be told where they get off if they go on acting like—like Belgian slave drivers in the Congo."

"All!" jeered Mark. "Anyway, the South isn't all—"

"Now listen, Mark. Is there *any* other civilized country in the world that would allow a gang of murderous morons like the KKK to terrorize people, and to get back into power after it'd been totally discredited once?"

"You know, children," said Charles Reilly, "this is something I like about the States. You do take politics seriously. Same as Ireland. I mean, ordinary intelligent people do, not politicians,

God help us—to them it's a game, a rough, tough, sophisticated game, like poetry is to poets."

"That's a very interesting point of view," said Chester, his eyes on the road ahead. "But don't *you* take poetry seriously?"

"Oh, *it's* not a point of view, it's the trut'. And will I tell you another thing?"

"Tell on," said Mark.

"I talked to a fella when I was reading down at Charlottesville—a good liberal Southerner. Oh, they do have them there, Sukie. He said he and many of his students *think* liberal but can't get their feelings in line with their intelligence: they've inherited this long tradition from their forefathers, living among slaves and then emancipated Negroes. It's atavistic. They know it's wrong, out of date, but, you see, they can't help themselves, can't smooth out their inner conflict."

"No, no!" Sukie exclaimed. "We know all *that*. But do you want us to wait politely till the South gets its emotions in phase with its intelligence? While human beings get lynched and bombed and treated like dirt there? There's a war on—a war of liberation?—or there should be, only all the fighting's done by the other side."

"A Maud Gonne come to judgment," murmured Reilly.

"Don't say that, Charles. She was hell on wheels, wasn't she? And I've got to marry *this* girl," protested Mark.

"This is a great girl, Mark my boy. If I had your age and my looks, I'd have stolen her from you."

And he probably would, thought Nigel, glancing round at Reilly's shock of red hair, his rosy face, brilliant blue eyes and sensual lips. Nigel had noticed, too, how serious had been Reilly's contribution to this fairly naïve political exchange: with his Irish empathy, he had adapted himself to what seemed to Nigel a basic rule of American conversation—one may be serious or frivolous, but never both in the same paragraph.

"Well, here we are," said Mark, "approaching the town of Amherst, the historical birthplace of America's greatest poetess or poet. It's behind a tall, tall hedge, I seem to remember."

"What is?" asked Chester.

"The birthplace, you dope." Sukie laughed. "Drive recklessly; we can't wait."

They entered the hilly town, its elegant frame houses spaced out among trees and sloping lawns. Presently Mark cried, "Left! You turn left here!"

Chester, who had overshot the crossing, did a hurried U-turn; and was instantly halted by a policeman on a motorcycle who had been following him. The officer poked his head in at the driver's window, and pointed silently to a notice at the roadside, which, in large letters, forbade U-turns.

"I'm terribly sorry," said Chester. "Now look, you don't want to give me a ticket. I'm really awfully sorry, I didn't see the notice. I *am* so sorry; you see, I overshot the intersection—"

The officer, after walking very slowly round the car to examine its registration plates, gave Chester a ticket. When the sordid procedure was over, Mark asked the man:

"Can you please tell us just where in this law-abiding town is located the birthplace of the great American poetess, Emily Dickinson?"

The man looked at him suspiciously, but could not think up any valid reason for bringing a further charge. He had to content himself with a piercing stare at Mark and a "never heard of her."

"Sure, they're all scared blue of the police over here," Reilly murmured to Nigel. "Now, did you ever hear anyone so apologetic?"

"That's because they're uncultured Irishmen and tote firearms," said Mark, who had overheard him. "Hey, don't look so worried, Chester. It might have happened to anyone. Come on, forget your persecution mania."

"I do not have persecution mania. I am persecuted. That is quite different."

"Have it your own way, brother."

After they had cruised around awhile, Mark found the house. They walked up the sloping lawn toward it.

"Are you quite sure it's empty?" asked Chester apprehensively. "We don't want to go bursting in on—"

"Take it easy," Mark reassured him. "We're pilgrims. Pilgrims rate special treatment."

"Of course it is," Sukie, who had scampered ahead, called over her shoulder. In a clear, toneless voice she chanted

> "There's been a death in the
>   opposite house
> As lately as to-day.
> I know it by the numb look
> Such houses have alway.

"Just get a load of that numb look, will you?"

Empty it certainly was and securely locked, as Mark proved by trying each of the ground-floor windows in turn.

"D'you think that's the door she hid behind when her parents were having company?" asked Sukie, peering in. "It all looks so swept and garnished. Sort of impersonal."

"It's her poems she inhabits," Mark said gently. "And do you remember?—one Sunday she refused to go to church, whatever her father said, and they couldn't find her anywhere, and when they got back, there she was in the cellar in a rocking chair, rocking away. Do you know her work well, Mr. Strangeways?"

"She was one of my favorites, in Oxford, in the twenties."

"A terrible hit-or-miss lady she was," said Charles Reilly.

"Morbid too. She's a one got more kick out of corpses than anything. And she'd no respect for God at all at all. 'Papa up there' indeed!—the pert little madam."

"Oh, Charles!" protested Sukie.

"Oh, she'd a great turn of phrase. Like a precocious child. But sure she was no artist," Charles persisted.

Sukie's eyes flashed. "That's ridiculous. D'you know what she said?—'Art is a house which tries to be haunted.' "

"Did she now? Did she say that now?" Charles ruminated. "That's good. I like it. That's very good indeed. Very well, I'll not say a word more against her."

Nigel sat them down for a photograph on the front steps. Peering into the magnifying view finder, he saw the four of them, tiny and sharp, in brilliant color. Reading from left to right: Chester, Mark, Sukie, Charles. Chester, with his small neat face and small neat body, a tentative smile on the one, gray-green English tweeds on the other. Mark, larger, not so tidy, corduroy trousers and a blue sports jacket, smiling broadly out of a round face. The streamlined figure of Sukie, gray eyes, black hair, vivid as a cardinal bird in her scarlet skirt and white sweater. Charles Reilly, pushing out his sensual lips as if to shape a wisecrack or a line of verse.

"A historic photograph," said Nigel, happily unaware how the future would take up his innocent words.

They walked to the Amherst cemetery and found the family graves of the Dickinsons. Some misguided culture lover had twined the railings around them with artificial morning-glories.

Mark shook his head. "Will you *look* at this! It's nauseating! It's uncouth. It's a scandal. If there's one thing Emily couldn't have tolerated, it's artificial flowers."

Sukie wasted no words. She began stripping the offensive floral tribute from the railings.

"Oh, now, Sukie—" Chester looked uneasily round—"I *don't*

think you should do that. It's sacrilegious; and they don't belong to you."

"Don't be so stuffy, Chester. They're a desecration. Aren't they, Charles?"

"Whoever strung them up had a right to do it. And you've a right to remove them."

"Oh glory!—now he's getting gnomic." Sukie swathed the string of flowers round and round Mark's neck. "Now rid me of them. Under that tree will do." Her lithe body swung forward to Nigel. "Tell me *you* approve."

"I approve."

Her gray eyes were in no hurry to withdraw from his. Mark had disappeared with his trophy behind a yew tree.

"There's Edward Dickinson. Papa below. Poor Papa. So upright. Such a good citizen. So totally incapable of communication," Sukie pointed out.

"Like some other fathers," said Chester, a rueful quirk on his mouth.

"He just wanted them all to stay at home—for ever and ever." Sukie sighed, "And here they all are. Safe in their alabaster chambers. If he could have imagined the journeys Emily took from her little room over there—"

"But I thought she never—" began Chester.

"Spiritual journeys, poop."

"Right away to the outermost circumference," said Mark, who had just returned.

" 'The Outer—from the Inner Derives its Magnitude,' " Sukie quoted.

"And that reminds me—where and how soon are we going to eat?" said Reilly. "My inner, my inner is yelling for dinner."

"Oh, Charles, really!"

"You must learn to pronounce my name the correct way. Char-luss."

"Well, it *is* about lunchtime. Let's go to the Yankee Pedlar," said Chester. "It's pretty nice."

"Yes, we must show Charles—Char-luss—a genuine old colonial inn. It's cute. The waitresses wear eighteenth-century Puritan dress, and you can drink from yards of ale, and they serve you dishes—"

"Now wait a minute, my angel Susannah." Charles interrupted. "Wait while the elders get a word in. I do not expect food, in the civilized sense of the word, over here. All I ask is bare sustenance. As your distinguished poet put it, American meals are a general mess of imprecision of feeding."

Mark groaned. His brother looked bemused. Nigel found Sukie's eyes on him again, with the candid, rather ingenuous gaze of the American woman.

"The only things the *Irish* can cook are potatoes and soda bread," Chester was saying—a nervous attempt to get into the lighthearted mood of the others.

"Well, you may have something there," Charles replied pacifically. All three of them, Nigel noticed, treated Chester with a sort of compunction, as though he were a foreigner for whom special allowances should be made. And he seemed an especially complicated man, for, though evidently a good driver, twice on the road there he had done a foolish thing. Was Chester Ahlberg accident-prone? Nigel wondered. Hardly. The accident-prone show it in their driving even when there's not another car in sight, snatching their gear changes, overbraking, doing nothing rhythmically. . . . Well, Americans were perhaps different all around. He didn't understand them fully so far.

An hour later in the bar of the colonial-type restaurant, they were digging gobbets out of a huge round cheese, each vowing every gobbet must be his last or there would be no appetite left for dinner. Charles and Nigel were drinking Scotch and water, Chester and Sukie martinis, Mark was on his third bourbon.

"Why do they wear those goddam mobcaps?" inquired Mark truculently.

"Atmosphere, my love," said Sukie.

"Don't they know that in the late seventeenth century 'mob' was a cant word for a strumpet, drab, or whore?" Mark pursued.

"I expect they're comfortable," said Nigel soothingly.

"I don't like being served by waitresses wearing whores' caps—not in a fine old typical Puritan-type joint. I must find out if they are aware of the etymology of their goddam caps. Waitress!"

"Mark! You *mustn't!*" hissed Sukie.

"Madam," said Mark to the waitress, "could you enlighten our English friend here? He wonders are those caps you wear as comfortable as they are attractive."

"Oh, yes, sir, they sure are."

"I'm exceedingly obliged to you."

"You're very welcome."

Sukie flashed an angry look at Mark, but said no more. Yes, he is a clown, thought Nigel; an intelligent clown, who is wild not far beneath his academic surface, and could be dangerous. A rich man's son. A bit spoiled? Old New England family. Inbred? Kicking over the ancestral repressions?

Summoned into the restaurant, they chose their food.

Charles Reilly turned to Chester. "Now's the time to ask you—in this fine respectable place—What do you actually do in the Business School? Just what goes on there now?"

"There are courses in economics, management, salesmanship, commercial history, theory of exchange, the ethical aspect of business—all that kind of thing."

"Well, that's fascinating," commented Charles, without undue enthusiasm. "But come, Chester, can you *teach* people to be successful businessmen? Sure, it sounds to me like those courses in creative writing you have over here: if you want to be a creative writer, you'd best stay at home and start writing creatively."

"Like Emily Dickinson," said Sukie.

"Oh, that's quite different. Business and writing are not a bit alike. A writer has to be alone, I guess. But a business nowadays is a team, hopefully at least." A mildly fanatic gleam had appeared in Chester's eye. "Take a problem we're tackling in one of my seminars as of now. The students are divided into two teams; each team has the assignment to put on the market a new and novel deodorant. One man is in charge of production, one handles labor relations, another the area marketing angle, another the costing, and so on; and of course they all get together on the basic factor in the promotional context."

"And what might that be?" Charles Reilly purred.

"Why, the image of the product, of course."

There was an awed silence, broken at last by Sukie:

"Chester, you're letting your steak get cold."

"It's like one of those war games H. G. Wells invented," said Nigel. "Or a house party to choose Foreign Office candidates."

"The logistical aspect presents an ever-increasing complexity. But we're handing that over more and more to computers," Chester said, prodding his steak with his fork.

"Are you now?" said Charles. "I wish you'd find one to write my poetry for me."

Mark leaned back with a satisfied sigh. "What I can't figure out, Ches old fellow, is why you go on teaching. With all this know-how lodged in your massive brain, you could become a captain of industry, a Napoleon of commerce."

A shuttered look came over Chester's face.

"I mean it, I'm not ribbing you. Look at father."

Chester frowned. "He was the last of the individualists. It's all teamwork now, from the white-coated men in the laboratory to the board room of the giant syndicate—"

" 'From Greenland's icy mountains to India's coral strand,' " bellowed Mark. "Say what you like, Ches, if I was father I'd stake you to a couple of million and take a side bet that you'd become another Rockefeller."

Chester blushed, looking secretive, and changed the subject to his forthcoming trip to Britain, where he was being consulted by the authorities of a new university about setting up a Business School there.

"Is your da all that rich?" asked Reilly. "Couldn't you prevail upon him to set up a foundation for indigent Irish poets?"

"Really, Charles! Why is it you Europeans are always begging?" said Chester, with unusual acerbity. "I mean—"

"What Chester means is that father'll use his dollars only for making jumbo-size public gestures," said Mark. "Like donating a fully equipped hospital to his home town, or building a new House at Cabot."

"Well," said Sukie, "if I was him, I'd subsidize the desegregation campaign—just buy up a few dozen Southern congressmen: they wouldn't cost him *all* that much—"

"Sukie, Sukie, how *can* you be so cynical at your tender age? Anyway, brother Josiah wouldn't approve your eating into his patrimony," grinned Mark.

"Josiah is a phony—a lousy, double-crossing rat. And you know it." Sukie's pretty, red mouth was distorted; she positively glared at Mark.

"My girl, you are speaking of the distinguished Homeric scholar? Can I believe my ears? Don't gorgonize me, pet: I am *not* his keeper."

"I should have thought *you*'d have minded what happened to John, considering—"

"Now look, honey, we've had all this before." Mark lowered his voice and Nigel could not hear what was said.

He turned to Charles Reilly, and they shortly wound up in conversation about W. B. Yeats, whose centenary was to be celebrated the following year. Charles, in his most reductive idiom, started telling several damaging stories about the poet.

"None of you Irish writers seems able to say a kind word about him," protested Nigel.

"Of course we can't. Willie Yeats is too big for us. We have to cut him down to our size, I know that. Still and all, he was a bit of a cod. But mind this—he hated fanaticism in politics because he knew the fanatic, the capacity for hatred, in himself."

Charles fell silent and Nigel heard Chester saying, ". . . tell him to go and talk to Josiah next Thursday then. I'll have a word with him. But I can't promise anything, Sukie, you realize that?"

Nigel saw the girl touch Chester's hand gratefully. It was noticeable that she kept her face turned away from Mark. "A Maud Gonne come to judgment," Nigel remembered. A strange thought, considering how tiny she would have looked beside that larger-than-life Irish heroine: but there was the fanatic glint in Sukie's eyes, the humorlessness, and the decisive way she now rose, collected her belongings, said it was time to go home.

2 ☞ Cockroaches and Crusaders

Nigel eyed his hostess with mild misgiving. One could never be sure what May Edwardes would say next: her remarks came at one from unpredictable angles, and the spectacle of a person trying to fend off her faster deliveries was as depressing as that of a village batsman failing to deal with a Test-Match bowler. A classical story was still going the rounds in Hawthorne House. May liked the tutors to call her by her Christian name. An observant freshman at one of her parties, noting this, said, "May I get you a drink, May?" "Yes, thank you," she replied. "I will take some bitter lemon. And please feel quite free to call me Mrs. Edwardes."

The wife of the Master—it was unwise to address her as the Mistress—of Hawthorne House was a Scotswoman of distinguished family and considerable academic attainment: she kept the latter cunningly masked so as to open the more devastating fire upon unsuspecting strangers. Tonight, unbecomingly clad in coffee-colored silk, she appeared to be in a permissive state of mind.

"I hope you're comfortable in your rooms, Nigel."

"Very comfortable, thank you."

"No trouble with cockroaches?"

"No. Should I?"

"Well, you know Cabot is famous for its cockroaches, and we like to think we have the most plentiful supply here at Hawthorne. Earlier this term, just before you came over, that poor wee Chester found a stage army of them walking round and round his bedroom one night."

"How very unpleasant. What did he do?"

"Slept on the couch in the sitting room. They come up from the basement in search of diversion, you know, or just a little peace and quiet, maybe."

Nigel thought it might well be the latter. The hardiest cockroach would surely be intimidated by the whirl of undergraduate life on the subground floor all around the main quadrangle: the boiler rooms, laundry rooms, canteen and locker rooms, television rooms, table-tennis rooms, and the Lord knew what else. By skillful use of this underground complex a student, unless compelled to attend lectures, need never put his foot out of doors once the New England snow had set in.

"I suppose they *had* walked to meet Chester," said Nigel thoughtfully.

"I was not aware that cockroaches can fly."

"No, I mean someone might have put them there—an enemy hath done this thing, May."

"Oh, come now, Chester is not only his own worst enemy, he's his *only* one."

"So *you* feel he's not persecuted, he just has persecution mania? *He* appears to take the opposite view himself."

May Edwardes, who had been gazing ruminatively toward the other end of the drawing room, where the person in question was talking with a group of colleagues, laid a hand on Nigel's sleeve.

"Then he deceives himself. People are persecuted either for their faith or for their eccentricity. Chester, as a typical modern American, has neither the one nor the other." Her voice took on the slight boom which heralded her cultural pronouncements. The company fell silent. The silence continued. Mrs. Edwardes broke it. She bent forward and eyed Nigel solemnly. "Considering what I've heard of your background," she said, "tell me, do you read detective fiction?"

"Sometimes," said Nigel.

"I hope you are sound on it."

"Sound?" asked Nigel.

"As an art form."

"It's not an art form. It's an entertainment."

May nodded approvingly. "Excellent. I have no use for those who seek to turn the crime novel into an exercise in morbid psychology. Its chief virtue lies in its consistent flouting of reality: but crime novelists today are trying to write variations on *Crime and Punishment* without possessing a grain of Dostoevsky's talent. They've lost the courage of their own agreeable fantasies, and want to be accepted as serious writers." This seemed to annoy her.

"Still, novels that are all plot—just clever patterns concealing a vacuum—one does get bored with them. I can understand readers getting sick of blood that's obviously only red ink."

"I'd have thought that *you* at any rate would prefer that kind." She seemed hurt.

"Now, May, please! I didn't come to Cabot to—"

But she was in full cry. "Zeke told me you have got yourself mixed up with a number of unsavory cases."

"And Zeke also told you, my love," said the Master firmly, coming over to them, "that Nigel's unsavory past was not to be mentioned in the clean, wholesome atmosphere of Hawthorne House. I cannot have my students distracted from their courses by prurient curiosity about the seamier side of British life."

"But the methods of a private investigator should be highly instructive—"

"My dear May, the private investigator is *out*—in fact as well as in fiction. Crimes of violence can only be dealt with now by teams of professionals," said Nigel.

"So much the worse, if that means we have to rely on our city police here. They're corrupt to a man." She sighed.

"I guess we'd best break it up, before you land yourself in court for slander. Nigel, I would like you to know another Ahlberg—this one, Josiah?" The Master, an exceedingly tall man with a skull-like head, who seemed to add interminably to his length, like a snake, when he straightened out, led Nigel to another corner of the drawing room, where a middle-aged man was sprawled in his armchair, smoking a pipe and paying no attention to the rest of the company.

Josiah and Nigel said they were glad to know each other. Josiah had the neat, dry face common among classical scholars: he looked as if he had grown into his skin—every wrinkle was in place. But this appearance of sedateness was contradicted by the fidgety glance of his eyes.

"Well, what do you make of us?" he asked abruptly.

"I've not been here a week yet. Too early for generalizations," Nigel said.

"If you can't make generalizations in the first few days, you'll never make them."

"That's probably true. But I'm not a journalist."

"Uh-huh. And I suppose every goddam student in the place has asked you how Cabot compares with Oxford." Josiah puffed a cloud of smoke over Nigel's head.

"Quite a few. And they really seem to want to know."

"That is typical of the American student. He believes that indiscriminately sucking in information is equivalent to acquiring knowledge." The eyes rolled.

"I find them extremely well mannered."

"An Ivy League tradition," Josiah remarked sourly. "And, of

course, in the dining hall polite conversation is necessary to palliate the horrors of the food. You realize that our food is shot through tunnels by compressed air from a central kitchen?"

"Have you proof of this?"

"The proof is in the pudding, as they say." Ahlberg permitted himself a half chuckle. "And the hot air is generated by the President and the Heads of Faculties. But your glass is empty. What are you drinking?"

"Bourbon and water."

Josiah Ahlberg returned with full tumblers. "They're tearing one another to pieces just now about the Aims of Education. As if they were the first living men to notice that it ought to have an aim. General education versus specialized studies—you know the setup. Insane! All it means is that each Faculty wants to grab more dough and prestige for itself." Josiah gave Nigel an amiable snarl.

"But the Classical Faculty is above such low motivations?"

"My dear Strangeways, you were a classicist yourself, the Master tells me. You know the classics don't need prestige. They've trained the best minds through the centuries; they'd still be the best discipline, the best way to put bone into thinking—conceptual *and* practical thinking—if we gave them a chance."

"Your brother would hardly agree."

"Chester?" Josiah made a smirking grimace. "The Business School! Trying to make a gentlemanly discipline out of the pursuit of rogues and anarchists! Every successful businessman has been an anarchist, a pure self-seeker: they've got to the top *because* the rest of us keep the laws, or can't share their monomania for money."

"I was thinking of Mark," Nigel put in mildly.

Josiah narrowed his eyes. "Mark? His talents don't lie in the money-making direction. Very much the reverse."

"No, I meant he wouldn't agree with you that the classics are the best foundaton—"

"Oh, I see. Sure. English. Not content with going to bed with that softest of soft options, he tries to make a governess out of her."

"He seems quite able," said Nigel.

"He writes crappy little articles for pseudo-scholarly magazines, if that's a proof of ability. When I was at Harvard, we read books—English and American literature—because a gentleman naturally read such books, took them in his stride. We did not—" Josiah snorted—"we did not 'study English literature.' Any more than the Greek audience 'studied' Aeschylus. Fancy telling an intelligent fellow why and how he ought to like Shakespeare!"

"You're from the South, aren't you, Mr. Ahlberg?"

"From the South? Is that my accent or my reactionary views? Actually my mother *was* a Southerner. However, my father's *second* wife came from the Midwest."

"What do you think of Susannah Tate? I met her last Sunday with your brothers."

A positively distraught look appeared on Josiah's face, to be swept away the next moment.

"Susannah?" he said slowly. "Well now, she's something of a firebrand, I guess. Maybe she'll settle down when Mark marries her. *If* Mark marries her."

"Oh? Why shouldn't he? She's pretty enough."

Josiah looked uncomfortable. It could be just that academic Americans tended to fight shy of the kind of extramural gossip that was meat and drink to Oxford dons, thought Nigel.

"She is. But she does play the field a bit." Josiah glanced round uneasily, then lowering his voice said, "You know she had an understanding with Chester last term. I don't say she's—well,—a golddigger, but she's not a very balanced girl—there's bad blood in that family. I suppose you know that her father was one of the Hollywood directors who got into trouble during the McCarthy investigations."

"That wouldn't necessarily imply moral degeneracy on his part," suggested Nigel gently.

"Oh, no. No, it wouldn't. No." The wild vague look was on Josiah's face. He clearly did not want to pursue the topic.

The party was breaking up. Josiah, waving his pipe at Nigel, asked him to stop by any time he felt like a chat—his office was B.24, and he was usually working there till close on midnight, and the Master invited Nigel to stay behind for a nightcap.

Nigel and the Master had known each other well at Oxford but had seldom met since. Zeke had been a passionate oarsman in those days, and as a result got embroiled with a female tow-path harpy from whose clutches Nigel managed at last to extricate the naïve young American, thus earning his lifelong gratitude and providing material for one of Nigel's undergraduate bons mots: " 'Tis Pity he's an Oar."

"I saw you heavily engaged with Josh," said the Master. "I hope your classical training stood you in good stead."

"He seems a very anxious man. What's he so anxious about?"

"Well now, he's highly conscientious, you know. As a teacher."

"But not as a scholar, a first-class mind?" Nigel asked.

"I wouldn't care to judge: it's not my subject."

"Evasive as ever, Zeke. I suppose masters have to be diplomatic. Well, it's the impression I got. And he's an odd mixture of sour and sweet, isn't he?"

"He must have got the sweetness from his mother," said May, who was lying full length on the sofa. "His father's a pompous old brigand."

"Now, May!"

"Does he get on all right with his father?"

"So far as I know."

"He'd better," May put in. "With all that money coming to

him when the old man finally consents to honor the next world with his presence."

"What? You mean the other brothers are left out of the will?" Nigel asked.

"Oh, no." Zeke explained that, when the plans for building Hawthorne House were afoot, old Mr. Ahlberg had hinted at his testamentary dispositions. Josiah, his first wife's son, would receive half the estate, the remainder being divided between Chester and Mark in equal shares. If either of the latter 'displeased' him, his share would go to the university for scientific research."

"What about his second wife?"

"Dead," remarked May. "She couldn't abide living with him any longer. You can give me another drink."

The Master did so.

"But why should he expect the younger sons to displease him?" Nigel asked. "They seem quite inoffensive."

"Well, Mark was rather frisky as an undergraduate. Got into debt badly—and I heard rumors of something worse. But he's sobered down now, hopefully," the Master explained.

"The fact is," said May, "the old ruffian would jump at a chance to disinherit either of them. He was passionately in love with his first wife, so it seems, and that's rubbed off on Josiah. Particularly," she added, "as he killed her."

"*What?*"

"Motor accident. He got a fit of conscience about it—the first and last time his conscience gave him any trouble."

There was a respectful silence.

"Well, anyway," said Nigel at last, "he surely can't be expecting Chester to kick over the traces."

"I'm afraid he has very little respect for Chester," said Zeke. "He'd have liked one of his sons to go into business—"

"Provided that son was noticeably less successful than himself," said Mrs. Edwardes.

"You may be right at that, May. Anyway, poor Chester did what he thought his father would think the next best thing. But the old man looks on the Business School as a sort of playing at soldiers. He has no use for it; and Chester feels this very, very badly."

"Still, he's obviously good at his job—being called in by a British university," said Nigel.

"Chester's a dull, earnest fellow—just the sort of American to impress English university authorities," said May. "He's circumspect. He'd never make an advance without first guaranteeing himself a line of retreat."

"Do you suppose he made his advances to Sukie Tate on that method?" asked Nigel.

"Och, here we are gossiping like old women!"

"You are an old woman, my love," said Zeke, kissing her brow.

"Away with you!"

Zeke said, "We've never really figured out just what the situation was between Sukie and Chester. They were going around, certainly—"

"And then the dashing Mark snatched her up on his horse?" said Nigel. "But it doesn't seem like that at all. I've only spent a day with them, I admit, but I couldn't make out whether they're engaged or not. American sexual mores defeat me. Surely to God they know if they're engaged?"

"Now be sensible, Nigel. She's a young girl. Why can't she be taking a little time to make up her mind?"

"All right, May. But I'm wondering if her mind is really on Chester *or* Mark. She's such a crusader she may give them both the slip," said Nigel.

"How do you figure that out?" asked Zeke.

Nigel told them some of last Sunday's conversation. "And what's all this between her and Josiah? He seems *not* to like her."

He was aware of that silent intercommunication between a

long-married couple which does not even need a glance for them to convey it.

Zeke uncoiled from his chair, went to the mantel.

"Plagiarism, Nigel. Her brother."

"Her brother? He's an author?" Nigel asked.

"No, no. What you'd call cribbing in Britain. John Tate was one of Josiah's most promising graduate students. He lifted a chunk of an unpublished essay by Josiah and served it up as his own in a thesis." A look of melancholy came over the Master's face. "We had to fire him from the university, of course. Temporarily. He can return in a year or two if he behaves himself."

"I see. And Sukie takes his side? Did her brother admit it was plagiarism?"

"He couldn't hope to conceal it—he'd hardly altered a word of the original."

"Rather surprising if he's such a bright lad."

The Master fidgeted with an ornament on the mantel. "Well, *his* case was that the crucial ideas in the thesis were his own: he'd talked them over with Josiah, who pinched them for this article of *his*."

"Oh Lord!"

"You can say that again. It was a very unpleasant situation to deal with. Of course, it was a foregone conclusion. Josiah is a man of probity, whereas John—well, we hadn't always found him overly reliable in other matters." The Master sighed.

"If Josiah's article had not been published at the time, how did the examiners know the lad had pinched his ideas?"

"One of them told Josh how brilliant the thesis was, outlined some of the points John had made. So Josh smelled a rat and asked to see it at once."

"As John's supervisor, wouldn't he do so anyway?"

"Sure. But later."

"Sounds as if this John Tate was a crusader like his sister," Nigel suggested.

"A crusader? Whatever do you imply by that?" asked May sharply.

"Sounds as if he deliberately sought a showdown with Professor Ahlberg. Otherwise, wouldn't he have altered the wording of Josiah's article, enough to cover his tracks anyway? After all, with the close relationship you'd get between a student and his supervisor, it'd be excusable, inevitable, for some of the latter's ideas to have rubbed off on his pupil."

"And *what* would this crusade be in aid of?" The Master was frowning.

"To make sure that the right man got in first with his own ideas," Nigel suggested. "Have you compared the two documents, Zeke?"

"Certainly. And I'm a historian and accustomed, if I may say so, to weighing evidence."

"Now don't go stuffy on me, old friend. Forget that one was written by a professor, who has probity and tenure and all that jazz, and the other by a graduate student of questionable morality—forget all that and tell me which was the better essay."

"But now look—"

"Which was the more convincing in its arguments, the better structured, the more scholarly?"

The Master made a long pause. "Well, if you put it that way, John Tate's. But—"

"Okay, okay, that's what I wanted. You don't have to tell me all the arguments on the other side. Very likely John's just the more persuasive writer of the two, and set out Josiah's points better than he could himself. Has Josh published his article yet, by the way?"

"No, he told me he wanted to keep it awhile for further consideration."

"You're not going to dig it all up, are you, Nigel?" said May suspiciously. "I don't want Zeke to go through that trouble all over again: it nearly drove him to tranquilizers."

"Good God, no. I've come here for pure escape, and to take a peek at your Herrick manuscript. Don't worry."

But even the smallest mystery had about as much chance of survival where Nigel Strangeways was present as an ant in a cage of anteaters. . . .

The House was quiet as Nigel made his way across the court to his own staircase. But lights were on behind the shades of almost every room. Very different from the sounds of revelry that used to cleave the air at night in his own Oxford college in the old days. They were a serious lot here: except for the Saturday dances and the occasional outbreak after a university football game, the long evenings of the fall were given up to study.

A couple of undergraduates coming in through the main gate, which was open all night, gave him a polite "Hi, Mr. Strangeways." It was wonderfully agreeable to be living among the young, but with no obligations to them or to any curriculum.

The great tower of Hawthorne House loomed above him. Who had given it that name? Surely not the founder? Old Mr. Ahlberg did not sound like a reading man.

Nigel took out his key, and let himself into his rooms. Paneled walls, two armchairs, three hard chairs with the arms of Cabot University on them, a sofa, an almost empty bookcase, a letter from Clare, which had arrived after lunch, on the desk. Somewhere above, a gramophone was playing, only just audible to him, the fourth Brandenburg. Presently even this fell silent.

He opened *Henderson the Rain King* and started to read; but this admirable work failed to take his mind off the strange story of the professor of Classics and the graduate student. There were several other things he should have asked Zeke, but the Master was evidently reluctant to be pumped about an episode which still gave him pain.

The Ahlberg brothers . . . So unlike one another in character and appearance . . . It must be difficult to be the sons of a millionaire and a tough old tycoon at that, by all accounts. Yet none of them, not even Mark, had settled down to the life of a playboy, as might have been expected . . . If there was anything spoiled in them, any inherited vice or conditioned weakness, it was not apparent. Each was making his own way. . . .

Suddenly there was the sound of footsteps beneath, and a yelling, bawling voice shattered the calm.

"Food Man! FOOD MAN! Hot dogs! Coke! Coffee! . . ."

Nigel still, after a week of it, leaped nervously in his chair every time he heard the appalling racket. Punctually at 10:15 P.M. every night the Food Man cried his wares at Nigel's entrance. Students, who had dined at 6:30, rushed to fortify themselves against another hour of work. The Food Man was himself a student, who at the start of term had bid highest for the job and the modest profits it brought in—an example of private enterprise which would have shocked Oxbridge dons to the marrow. His bawlings could now be heard diminuendo as he went from entrance to entrance toward the far end of the court.

The only comparable din in this sedate home of learning was the bells of a neighboring house. They had been brought, apparently, from a derelict monastery in Russia, and had been set up in the great tower. And a derelict monk had been hired to come over and teach the undergraduates to ring them. Either the monk was past his work or the tradition had been lost during the thirty years since the bells had been hung; for the present team which rang them from 12:40 to 12:50 each Sunday morning, produced an extraordinary sort of campanological pandemonium: Charles Reilly had described it as "an avalanche of ironmongery falling from heaven, like Lucifer."

When the yells of the Food Man had at last died away, Nigel went to bed. He felt too sleepy to face the usual encounter with his shower—a treacherous mechanism which, after he had regulated it (standing well away) to the desired temperature, would suddenly emit scalding water when he was defenseless beneath it.

In bed, drifting toward sleep, he heard the distant wailing of a siren. It was either a fire engine or a rescue truck: he was not yet able to distinguish between the two sounds. He remembered Charles Reilly, who flatly refused to believe it was either rescue truck or fire engine which produced such uncanny howls, saying, "It's a banshee, Nigel, and you know what that means. A death in the House. You'd think they'd be more nervous."

3 ☞ The Spooky Treasure Hunt

Sometime during the next five days Charles Reilly's gloomy prognostication did in fact come true, though nobody was aware of it because nobody missed the victim.

It was not till the Monday after the Edwardes' party that any uneasiness began to be felt in Hawthorne House, where, if a Faculty member's office door bears a notice saying "All appointments canceled for next few days," the docile undergraduate accepts it and carries on with his assignments. The more demanding students, if there were any, would have knocked on the door, and receiving no answer, have gone away.

Nigel, coming in to lunch on Monday, sat down at a table beside Mark and Charles, who were already in conversation.

". . . well, I haven't seen him lately," Mark was saying.

"It's a damned nuisance. He asked me to dinner, and I can't remember was it for today or tomorrow. Hello there, Strangeways. I rang up his office, and his apartment. Twice. No answer. Where else would I try?"

"The Faculty building perhaps."

"Did he say he was going away anywhere for the weekend?"

"Not to me."

"Whom are you talking about?" asked Nigel.

"Josiah."

"Better try his apartment again after lunch," suggested Mark. "His cleaning woman comes in the afternoon."

"Would he have gone off for the weekend with a woman, and be wanting to keep it dark?" Charles Reilly's blue eyes twinkled.

"Oh, come. I am not my brother's keeper," said Mark, "but I guess that is about the unlikeliest thing in the world."

When they had finished their meal they went first to Josiah's office on the first floor of B entry, and saw the notice.

"That's peculiar," said Mark.

"He doesn't often cancel appointments?" Nigel asked.

"No. He's a conscientious s.o.b. I'll give him that."

"No date on it, either," said Nigel.

"Why don't we go in?" asked Reilly. "The fella might have been lying dead on the floor for days."

Mark looked at him. Then his hand went toward his pocket, stopped halfway, then moved on and took out a pack of cigarettes. "We'll ask the Superintendent for the spare key, maybe. But let's try Elsa first."

Elsa, the Negro cleaning woman, whom Mark rang up, said that Mr. Ahlberg had not slept at home since Wednesday night, and had left no message for her: letters were beginning to accumulate in the mailbox. Josiah, Mark told Nigel and Charles, had a bed in his office and sometimes slept there if he had been working late.

Finally they fetched the spare key from the Superintendent in the gate lodge, and returned to B entry. Mark inserted the key and gently opened the door.

It was an austere room, a few yellowing prints of Greek antiquities on the brown-paneled walls, a filing cabinet, a desk with a carpet under the desk chair—the usual office fittings—a low bookcase filled with classical texts all round the walls.

Its usual occupant was not there. Nigel poked his nose into the small washroom next door. This too was empty. Mark was riffling through the papers on the desk. "No message here," he said.

"What's this?" Nigel pointed to a large, squared worksheet pinned to one of the walls.

"That's Josh's schedule of seminars and individual pupil appointments for the term."

"And the ticks in red ink?"

"He makes them at the end of each tutorial period: if any student fails to turn up, he puts his initials in the appropriate square. Why?"

"There are no ticks after Thursday last," Nigel said. "He had appointments for Friday, but they are not ticked. So he must have put that notice on the door on Thursday night or early Friday morning."

"And then vanished into thin air, leaving not a wrack behind," remarked Charles, pushing out his thick lips. "So what do we do next?"

"Obviously we ask the Master," said Nigel. "Josiah may have got leave of absence for a few days, for private reasons."

But Zeke had received no such request from the professor—indeed, had not set eyes on him since the night of the party.

At this stage, however, though mildly mystified, neither he nor Nigel was worried. . . .

Cabot University, albeit a civilized place, preserved a few faint traces of the ferocious ordeals through which freshmen used to be put in the bad old days. One such in Hawthorne House, its secret jealously guarded by the sophomores who managed it—and known to every Faculty member from the Master downward—was the "spooky treasure hunt." The freshman was instructed to proceed at dead of night to some cryptically indicated point, usually in the capacious bowels of the House, where he would find an object which must be conveyed at breakfast next morning to the sophomore committee. The object, whatever else it might be, was always a bizarre and sometimes a revolting one.

Dennis Goach knew this from an older brother who had been in the House, and was prepared for the worst. At midnight on Monday he was stealing cautiously, torch in hand, through the dark basement passages. An intelligent youth, he had correctly interpreted the clue as directing him first to a disused locker room. He had, by the exercise of considerable guile, overcome the first hurdle, which was to "borrow" the key of this locker room from the Superintendent's office.

Arrived now at its door, he inserted the key and turned. The door would not open. He turned it back and tried the handle again. This time the door did open—with a faint screech of hinges: it had never been locked. Dennis threw the torchlight round the room. Tall, vertical lockers lined it all the way round, faded names marked on some in white chalk. The lad stood still for a moment, holding his breath, half expecting some spooky manifestation, but no bloodcurdling howl from the ordeal-mongers rent the air. He was about to direct the torch back upon the piece of paper containing the clues when he became aware of a curious smell in the room.

Now Dennis had been expecting the "treasure" he was seeking to be something repellent—a dead rat, maybe. So he followed his nose round the lockers till he came to one where the stench was most noticeable. He seized its knob, thinking he might well find it locked, in which case he would have to break it open somehow. But he encountered no such difficulty. The locker opened easily, and a large dummy fell out of it, accompanied by a gust of atrociously foul air. At least, he assumed it to be a dummy, until he shone the torch at what lay on the wooden floor, and perceived it to be Professor Ahlberg, with a neat round hole in his temple.

Whereupon Dennis Goach went into a light faint. Coming to

consciousness after a minute, he got onto hands and knees beside the carrion thing, and was violently sick. . . .

A few minutes later the Master, on his way upstairs to bed, heard a loud hammering on the front door of his lodgings. He hurried down and opened, to find a white-faced undergraduate there.

"Dennis? What in heaven's name—?"

"It's Mr. Ahlberg!" (Dennis was not so sick as to forget the Cabot tradition that all professors are called "Mister.") "He's dead. In the locker room. I found him."

"Good grief! Here, Dennis, you look all in. You must have some brandy."

"But—"

"Take it easy. Are you sure he's dead? Okay, then, the poor fellow can keep for a minute."

"He hasn't kept very well, sir," blurted Dennis rather hysterically, and was at once appalled by the bad taste of his observation. "I'm sorry   "

"Hold it! Drink this."

Dennis did so. When the brandy had brought a litttle color into his cheeks, the Master asked, "What on earth were you doing down in the locker room at this time of night? We don't use it any more—didn't you know that?"

"Well," Dennis replied uncomfortably. "It was a sort of—" He broke off, remembering his vows of secrecy.

"A sort of—? Oh, a sort of ordeal? That tomfool treasure hunt. Well, forget it. I want you to go and rouse the Superintendent. Send him to the locker room. Tell him to switch on all the basement lights. Wait a minute—and rouse up Mr. Strangeways too. D. 32. Hustle!"

When Nigel arrived there with Dennis, the lights were blazing in the locker room. The Master and stocky Mr. Gross, the Superintendent, were standing at some distance from the object on the floor, gazing helplessly down at it. Nigel went up and gave one glance at the drilled, blackened forehead, the corner of the mouth twisted in that familiar snarl.

"Shot. Small-caliber weapon. Quite effective, though, if fired close up, as this obviously was."

"Now why in the Lord's name should Josh want to shoot himself?" the Master asked.

"He didn't. You found him in there, Mr. Goach, you said?" Dennis nodded dumbly.

"Where's the weapon? Not in that locker. Not on the floor. Oh, no, he was shot and put in there."

"But, Nigel—" the Master almost bleated.

"When was this room last cleaned out, Mr. Gross?"

"In the vacation, sir."

"So he was shot somewhere else. But of course he was, Zeke. Look! No blood on the floor, none in the locker. You've telephoned the police?"

"I did," said Mr. Gross. "Before I came along here."

"Good. We must leave it to them now. Try not to touch any surface here."

"Shall we lock the door and wait for them upstairs?" asked Zeke.

"Could I say something?" asked Dennis.

Nigel glanced at the boy's intelligent face. "Go ahead."

"The door—the room door—was not locked when I came in. I—er—had a key, but it wasn't needed."

"You had the key?" said the Superintendent menacingly. "How—?"

"Never mind about that," Nigel said. "Was the door usually kept locked?"

"I guess not. Nothing here to steal nowadays."

"When did you last inspect the room?"

"Two—three weeks ago I looked in," said Gross, looking disgruntled.

"But you expected to find it locked, Mr. Goach?"

"Well, I somehow assumed it would be."

"You were instructed to pinch the key as part of the ordeal?" inquired the Master.

Dennis was saved from having to reply by the distant sound of a police-car siren. They hurried along the passages and up the stairs into the main gate lodge. . . .

"Grilled me? Sure, they grilled me," Dennis was saying to a group of friends at breakfast next morning. "For an hour."

"Right there in front of the cadaver?"

"Don't be a dope. In the Master's lodge."

"So you're the chief suspect."

"I'm the man who is assisting the police in their investigations."

"They say the third degree is very, very painful."

"It's the only degree Dennis'll ever get."

"Majoring in homicide. Boy, oh boy!"

"Aw, drop it, won't you?" protested the much-tried youth. "Let's call it a day."

"Sic transit gloria mundi."

"What's this guy Strangeways doing, getting mixed up in it?"

"He's a British private investigator, staying here incognito."

"Going to save you from the chair, is he?"

"Al, you kill me."

"What is your chief impression of the slaying, Mr. Goach? Off the record, of course."

"The pong," Dennis said.

"What's that again?"

"Pong. British word for stench. 'Thank God to get out of that pong,' Strangeways said when we left the locker room."

Al savored it. "Pong. A good word, professor. An excellent word. I like it. In future, let it supersede all other synonyms." . . .

"No, no, Zeke, I'm not getting mixed up in this affair." Nigel was breakfasting with the Master, gummy-eyed with sleeplessness. "That lieutenant is a perfectly competent chap, so far as I could judge."

"But, Nigel, you've already got yourself involved. All I'm asking you is to keep an eye on things, from the House's angle—as my representative."

"The whole place is seething with cops. I'm just not butting in on them. Not even for you."

The Master shrugged, and addressed himself to his egg. Nigel was voraciously consuming toasted corn muffins, for which he had developed a passion.

"I suppose there's no doubt he was shot in his office," said Zeke presently.

"Not much. All those bloodstains they found under the mat. I presume the murderer shot him at or near his desk, and pulled the mat over the stains before carting him down to the basement."

"Why not just leave the body in the office?"

"A cleaner—anyone with a key—might have come in. He wanted to gain time." Nigel chewed thoughtfully. "But for Dennis' carry-on, the body might have stayed in that locker for weeks or months."

"What I can't understand is how nobody in Josh's entry heard the shot."

"Oh, that's easy," Nigel absently replied. "Do you have any more muffins?"

"Easy! What, for Pete's sake, do you mean?" asked Zeke, ringing for a fresh supply.

"There are two points of time," said Nigel, swinging into his dogmatic vein, "when anyone conversant with the routine of your House could feel quite safe about letting off a pistol."

"Is that so?" said Zeke skeptically.

"It is. One, on Sunday when those goddam bells are ringing. Two, when the Food Man starts screaming the place down. Either would drown the noise of a pistol. I assume it to have been the latter, because Sunday morning is no time to be toting bodies around. The killer would be in Josiah's office already, talking to him. When the Food Man starts bawling, he whips out his gun and fires."

The Master stared at Nigel. "Say, does the Lieutenant realize this?"

"He's only to ask anyone who lives here. Anyway, it doesn't help all that much. We can guess the time of day, but we don't know *which* day. And I doubt if the autopsy will be able to fix it with any certainty. Ah, here are the muffins. A little more butter would be in order."

Zeke passed the butter. "Lieutenant Brady has an appointment with me in half an hour. I'd very much like you here to support me."

"No fear," said Nigel, his mouth full. "I'm going to bed when I've finished these. I can't think without sleep."

"You know, Nigel, I am very deeply distressed about poor Josiah."

"I know."

"I feel ashamed to be worrying about how this is going to upset the routine of the House, when—"

" 'Drive your cart and your plough over the bones of the dead'—it's a harsh saying, but it's the best we can do." . . .

"Am I speaking to Bentham's Hotel? . . . Will you put me through to Mr. Ahlberg's room? Mr. Chester Ahlberg." . . .

Mark lodged the receiver under his chin and lit a cigarette. The long-distance call to London had been expeditiously obtained.

"Chester? This is Mark. Look—I—I have some sad news for you. Can you hear me well? . . . Ches, listen, Josh has been found dead . . . Yes, dead. What's that? . . . Well, I telephoned you as soon as I could, he was only found last night . . . Yes, around midnight. They didn't tell me till five A.M. . . . In that old locker room in the basement . . . I know it's crazy . . . He'd been shot and his body was stuffed into a locker . . . No, we don't know, the police may by now . . . Yes, I'm trying to contact father, but he's in Bermuda and I don't have a number for him . . . You'll fly back today if you can get a reservation? Okay. Good. Fine."

Mark picked a strand of tobacco off his tongue, and dialed Sukie.

"Honey, it's me. I can't meet you for lunch, we've had a horrible thing happen. It's Josiah. He was found dead last night. Shot . . . No, no, not suicide . . . Now take it easy, Sukie, don't get so worked up about it; after all—he wasn't your favorite, now, was he? You don't have to— Okay, honey, I'll be along just as soon as I can make it."

Mark stared out unseeingly at the ivy crimsoning on the neo-Georgian buildings across the court. Death produced strange responses, he thought: both Sukie and Chester had reacted strongly, but not at all in the ways he would have expected. He himself seemed to feel no reactions at all. Maybe he was just callous—or in shock still. He found it curiously difficult to remember how he'd felt toward Josiah when he was alive. His face twitching a little, he reached for the day's teaching schedules on his desk, then pushed them aside, realizing there was no chance of the usual routine's operating today. Glancing out the window again, he saw the athletic figure of Lieutenant Brady striding toward the Master's lodging, two bulky plainclothes men behind him. . . .

Aside from the inevitable tickets from traffic cops, Ezekiel Edwardes had had no brushes with policemen since certain discreditable episodes on Guy Fawkes night at Oxford. He was aware that the Master of a House at Cabot has not the almost godlike autonomy of the head of an Oxford college. So it was a relief to find that Lieutenant Brady behaved in a civilized, an almost respectful, way. He did not even chew gum or gnaw at an extinct cigar.

"They gave me this assignment," said the Lieutenant, smiling faintly, "because they decided I'm less of a roughneck than some of my colleagues."

Zeke felt himself blushing to have his thoughts so instantaneously put into words. Annoyed with himself, he sought refuge in his authority.

"I should be happy to know, Lieutenant, how your investigations are proceeding. Can you tell me yet when my students and instructors will be able to resume their normal avocations?"

"Certainly, Master. My men have to search every apartment for the weapon, and interview members of your House." Brady explained that the search was radiating outward from the dead man's office.

"Do you mind if these two fellows search your own lodgings now?"

Nonplused, Zeke agreed. "Though I wouldn't care to say what my wife will think about it."

"Thanks. Get it over with." Brady grinned pleasantly. "Just where a killer would cache his gun. In detective novels. The unlikeliest place, huh?"

Brady asked the Master to have the students assembled in the dining hall after lunch: he would start a preliminary general inquiry from there. "It's strange," he said, frowning, "that no-body on Mr. Ahlberg's staircase should have heard a shot."

"Oh, that's easily explained. Not my idea—Mr. Strange-ways'," Zeke added hurriedly, and put forward Nigel's hypothesis.

"Sounds reasonable to me. Who is this guy Strangeways? Some sort of amateur criminologist?"

"Yes. But he doesn't want to get mixed up with the police."

"Who does?"

Who indeed, thought Zeke, miserably aware of the unnatural life which had broken out in his quiet House, all the homicide men swarming behind the ivy-covered walls. The—what was that line—"the consternation of the ant-hill"?

Seated in the dark-blue leather armchair, Brady eyed him patiently. "You're wondering when I'm going to ask the ten-thousand-dollar question?"

"The—? I'm not with you."

"What enemies did Mr. Ahlberg have? Was he a popular in-structor?"

"Well, I wouldn't quite say that, Lieutenant. A thoroughly respected one, though," Zeke added hastily.

"By everyone? . . . You have something on your mind, Master. Anything happened recently you want to tell me? Did he get along with his colleagues?"

So the story of John Tate and the plagiarism was eased out of Ezekiel Edwardes. "But," he concluded earnestly, "John's no murderer, believe me. A bit anti-authority at times. But he's a good lad at heart. I just couldn't credit it that he'd creep back here with a gun and—he might have struck Josh, in a rage, when first—"

"Okay, okay, let's not make a production of it. Do you have his present address, and a photograph maybe?"

"My secretary will give you his last known address. There's a group photograph, but I daresay his sister would be more help to you." Zeke pressed a button on his desk and gave the secretary instructions.

"Ahlberg have any woman trouble?"

The Master gave Brady a quelling look, which bounced off his hard, intelligent face. "Certainly not, so far as I'm aware. We think—we've always thought Mr. Ahlberg a confirmed bachelor."

"How about the dough then? Who stands to get it?"

Zeke was beginning to revise his first opinion of the Lieutenant's social graces. "You'll have to ask Mr. Ahlberg's lawyer about that," he coldly replied.

"Oh, I will, I will, Master. He has two brothers in the university, right?"

"That is so."

"No family ructions?"

"Not that I know of. You'd better ask Mark Ahlberg." The Master's eye was frosty. "Firsthand evidence is always, I find, the most valuable."

"But not necessarily always true. What about the other one?"

"Chester? He's been in Britain since Thursday last. Mark is telephoning him to return."

"Well, I must be on my way. I'm grateful for your cooperation." Lieutenant Brady gave his sudden, winning smile. "And I understand your reluctance to talk, Master. Nobody likes shooting off his mouth about his friends."

When May came in five minutes later, Zeke was staring absently into a cup of cold coffee.

"What on earth are those men doing, tramping about upstairs?"

"Looking for the gun Josh was killed with."

"Well, for mercy's sake! *Here*?"

"Nothing is sacred to a homicide squad, my dear. Not even a master's lodgings."

"And any moment we'll have the crime reporters down on us."

"I've briefed the senior tutor to give them a statement. If they succeed in getting past Lieutenant Brady. He's a formidable character, I fancy. I do wish Nigel would show some interest," Zeke added pettishly. *"He* said he was going off to bed."

"And that's the best thing you can do, too."·

4 ☞ When Did You Last See Your Brother?

That same night, after dining alone in a restaurant, Nigel found a message from Mark slipped under his door. He went across to Mark's rooms, where Charles Reilly was already established, with a glass of whisky at his side.

"Come on in now," Charles welcomed him. "We badly need you for the post-mortem."

"Have you heard the results?"

There was an unhealthy pallor over Mark's sallow skin. "They can't pin it down precisely. But they seem to think my brother died on Thursday night or Friday morning."

"Which means Thursday night," said Nigel.

"At any rate, when Lieutenant Brady had us all assembled in the hall after lunch, no one had seen Josh on the Friday morning. Bourbon all right for you, Nigel?"

"Thank you. . . . Anything else come of the meeting?" Nigel asked idly.

"You're damn right it did. Brady asked who'd been near Josh's entry that night, aside from the fellows who room there—he'd already interviewed *them*, it seems."

"Yes?"

Mark took a gulp of his drink. "One fellow—young Bronsky—said he'd seen me coming away from there about 10:15."

"And had he?"

"He had. So I'm in the doghouse."

Reilly's brilliant blue eyes were fastened on Mark. Nigel said nothing.

"Well, aren't you going to ask me about it?" Mark irritably broke out.

"It's none of my business. If you want to talk about it, though—"

"I thought you were interested in hunting criminals." Mark's tone was at once pettish and provocative.

"Why, you're not a criminal, are you, Mark?" said Nigel mildly.

"The way *they* act—one of Brady's gorillas spent an hour this afternoon examining my clothes. For bloodstains."

Nigel was silent.

"He didn't find any. And it can be proved I sent nothing to the laundry today." There was a note of near-hysteria in Mark's voice, though.

"Go on, boy, tell him, tell him," said Charles. "He's one of these dumb Englishmen."

"I had a note from Josh—typewritten, with his initials scrawled on it—asking me to come and see him in his office at 10:15 on Thursday night. I went there, knocked on his door, no reply. So I came away. Period. Just period."

"You'd destroyed the message, of course?" asked Nigel automatically.

"Sure I destroyed it. I don't keep odd bits of paper lying around. Why should I?"

"What's your worry then?"

Mark's mouth twitched. "When Brady interviewed me this morning, I didn't tell him about this. Why should I? I hadn't heard or seen anything suspicious when I went along to the office."

Charles Reilly pushed out his lips in a considering way. "You made a mistake there."

"I *know* I did. But—"

"Has it been established," Nigel broke in, "when the Food Man came to your brother's entrance?"

"About 10:08."

"So you missed him by seven minutes. The murderer had either got rid of the body before you turned up, or he was still in the office when you knocked. Why didn't you let yourself in?"

Mark stared at Nigel. "How in hell would I do that without a key?"

Nigel had not failed to notice the half-movement toward his pocket which Mark had made yesterday morning outside Josiah Ahlberg's door. But he answered:

"I mean, tried the doorknob. Your brother was expecting you, so you thought. Might he have left the door unlocked?"

"You didn't know my brother," said Mark bitterly. "He guarded his privacy from us all."

"He was a bloody man, right enough, God rest his soul," said Charles easily.

"Now, I don't like to hear you say that. You needn't say that!"

"It can't hurt him, Mark. It can only hurt me, and I'm as hard as a bag of horseshoes."

"I rather liked him," said Nigel. "Why do you say he was a bloody man, Charles?"

"Oh, Mark has told me about the way he treated him and Chester when they were boys. I've heard all about it. Let alone the way he went talebearing to their father when—"

"Oh, *I've* forgotten all that," Mark said.

"You have not, Mark. You may have forgiven it—that's another matter. It's your duty to forgive, and you can't forgive what you've forgotten."

"Oh, to hell with your sanctimonious Jesuitical logic chopping!" exclaimed Mark without anger. It relieved the thunderous atmosphere which had been building up in the room. Charles Reilly grinned amiably at the two of them.

"Sorry. Sorry. The trouble with Americans," he propounded, "is that there's no give in them. They're so formal and inhibited that, when something happens to knock them off their beautifully laid tracks, they're helpless as overturned beetles. The English, on the other hand, don't run on rails at all. They're romantics, who conceal their romanticism by behaving half the time like buffoons—will you listen to me, Nigel? You sit there as deaf as a haddock—"

"I was admiring your Celtic flair for mixed metaphors."

"The mixed metaphor, like the so-called Irish bull, is a sign of exceptional imaginative dash. But leave that be. What are we going to do about young Mark here?"

"Do?"

"Him with his brother dead and he's under suspicion from the police as well."

"They don't often charge innocent people," Nigel said.

"May God help you!"

"They have no grounds for suspicion except a perfectly trivial coincidence—" Nigel said patiently.

"May I be allowed to horn in on this discussion?" said Mark.

"By all means." Charles waxed expansively. "What Mark is going to tell us is that he has a motive for the crime. With his brother out of the way, he stands to gain that much more when his father dies. I mean, that is how the Homicide Department will see it."

"So?" Nigel asked.

"Well, for the Lord's sake, Nigel, don't sit there like a constipated owl on a rooftree swigging the fellow's liquor. Which reminds me, my glass appears to be empty. . . . Thank you, Mark. What was I saying?"

"That Mark has a motive. So has Chester."

"But *I* wasn't in Britain when it happened," Mark protested. Nigel barely heard him. "So have plenty of others, for all I know. Students, the Senior Tutor, the Master, Charles here, any instructor in the House—or outside it—you all seem to be able to wander in and out quite freely any time of day or night. We can do nothing till we know what concrete evidence the police turn up. Motives are *not* concrete evidence."

"But motive," said Charles, "must modify their attitude toward the concrete evidence. And forewarned is forearmed."

"I don't consider that last a very meaningful proposition," said Mark.

"Listen, my boy. Just you *listen*. Knowing *they* know you have a motive, we must anticipate any attempt by Brady to tailor the evidence to fit it."

"You mean we've got to cook the evidence?" asked Mark. "Oh, really? *What* evidence, anyway?"

Oh God, thought Nigel, here we go. Academic circles are too damned articulate, too bright altogether. These sorts of people would talk their way into the dock if they didn't get there by conventional means. What on earth is Brady going to make of them, all talking away like books and acting like mental defectives? And why is Charles Reilly so keen to get himself embroiled—loyalty to Mark? mischievous curiosity? just a simple desire to be in the middle of any conflict that arises?

Light feet were running up the stairs. Mark opened the door as a fist beat on it. Sukie ran straight in—into his arms, and out of them, almost pushing him away.

"They're after him!" she panted.

"Take it easy, honey. After whom?"

"John, of course." She burst out crying, and fell into a chair. Charles eyed her attentively.

"You'd better have a drink, my dear." He poured out a neat Scotch. She took a gulp, then slammed the tumbler down on the table beside her.

"He was at me for hours—a horrible lieutenant—calls himself Brady. When did I last see John? When did I hear from him last? What address did I have for him?" Her eyes blazed behind the tears. "Who told him about John and your brother? Who? I'll kill the rat who told him!" she exclaimed with shrill violence. "They've had it in for my family ever since dad had that trouble with that McCarthy swine."

"Now look, Sukie, it was bound to come out—the row between your brother and Josh—"

"You mean *you* told Brady?" Her voice was like splinters of ice.

"I *certainly* did not." Mark's pale face was flushed. "I've been too busy defending my own reputation."

"And what did you answer?" Nigel spoke quietly, and it seemed to calm the overwrought girl.

"Answer?"

"To Brady's questions."

Nigel seemed to intercept a glance from her to Mark.

"I haven't seen John for weeks. He's not allowed back at Cabot. And he doesn't write much. When I last heard, he was in Pittsburgh, doing a lousy factory job."

"Well, now, isn't that a shame—John not even writing when you and he were so close," said Charles Reilly.

Sukie went on: "And d'you know, Brady stole his photograph off my desk?"

"Stole?" Nigel asked.

"Took it, abstracted it, walked off with it."

"Surely he gave you a receipt?"

"What if he did? I told him not to take the photograph. I dare say the Nazis gave receipts for all the paintings they looted out of—"

"Whisht, my dear." Charles's voice was double Irish cream. "We have a rescuer in our midst. This is Nigel Strangeways, the great criminologist, who is going to melt all our troubles away. Be easy."

"I'm damn well not going to," Nigel said.

"Ah, you couldn't refuse a gerrul with eyes like Connemara—"

"Don't come the Paddy-Irish over me, Charles."

"But you will? Say you will!" Sukie seized Nigel's forearm with a febrile grasp.

"But look here—" Nigel protested.

"Please," said Mark.

"Will you *listen,* you children! I know nothing about American police methods, I have *no* standing with the police here: if I poked my nose in—"

"Which," interrupted Charles, "you're dying to do."

"Shut up!—They'd bloody it for me, and quite right too. Furthermore, I hardly know any of you—"

"Let me introduce us—" Charles began.

"I've not been here a fortnight yet. And I *don't yearn to hear* all your squalid secrets. However—"

"Oh, bless you, Nigel," cried the girl.

"I'm always willing to talk to Sukie—say tomorrow at midday. If she will remember that I take nobody's part yet in this. And *if* she decides to tell the truth. Thanks for the drinks, Mark. I'm for bed. Good night." . . .

Nigel put down his book and went to the window. He gazed out at the trees in the courtyard, down to the grass beneath them where gray squirrels darted about erratically and pigeons pecked. A blue jay stalked among them, giving vent to an occasional raucous squawk as unpleasing as its color was delightful. Overhead, the sky maintained its uniform blue, uninterrupted by a single cloud, and a shuttle plane to New York slid past, filling up the sky like a bowl with sound.

Policemen stood talking together at each of the two gates that came within Nigel's vision. Students, released to their normal tasks, brushed past them, carrying their books in canvas bags. They look so young, thought Nigel: can I ever have been as young as that? There is a firm intention in their walk—they neither saunter nor run, as we used to do, enjoying our brief spell of freedom between school and job: they are already seriously committed to the future. Will that girl turn up?—I doubt it. Do I want her to?—who knows?

But at five past twelve he saw Sukie coming across from the direction of Mark's rooms, walking with the long, strangely sexless stride of the American girl, scattering before her the pigeons and squirrels, ignoring the beautiful jay.

"Sorry I'm late," she said, unslinging the bag from her shoulder, "my supervisor kept me."

Well, Mark Ahlberg *is* her adviser on the Emily Dickinson thesis.

Sukie arranged herself on the sofa—supple, small body, gray eyes, long black lashes. She looked round her:

"My, what an austere apartment! You should borrow a picture or two from Chester."

"I'm only here for a few weeks. It's hardly worth dressing the place up."

"Do you have a nice home in London?"

"Yes. Early Georgian. In Greenwich, near the Thames."

"But you don't really mind where you live, do you? You live in your mind, I guess."

"Only some of the time," he answered, smiling. "Like you."

"Oh." She frowned a little, her fingers lacing and unlacing in her lap. "I'm nervous of you."

"Well, let's make conversation a bit longer, then."

There was a pause, in which she seemed to be trying to screw up her courage.

"Chester's back," she said finally.

"Oh, yes?"

"He flew in early this morning. Now he's sleeping it off, Mark says. Chester can't sleep on an airplane."

Another silence. "Would you care for some bitter lemon?" he asked. "It's rather good at this time of day, with a drop of gin."

Sukie nodded. While he poured out the drinks, his back turned, she asked abruptly, "Why did you say 'if she decides to tell the truth'?"

"Because you hadn't told it, Sukie." He kept his back turned, to embarrass her less.

"About what?" she temporized.

"Your brother."

"Oh, what do you mean?"

Nigel gave her a glass. "In the restaurant that Sunday, Chester said to you, 'Tell him to go and talk to Josiah next Thursday.' You were talking about John, weren't you?"

"My, do you have total recall?" she asked in a brittle voice.

"But you told Brady you hadn't seen him for weeks."

"That slob! But I hadn't either."

"Oh, Sukie, Sukie!"

"No, it's *true*."

"You mean, he came here last Thursday without seeing you?"

The long black lashes came down over her eyes. "I don't know whether I can trust you," she broke out at last, in an agonized voice.

"But you have to, don't you?" he replied gently.

Sukie looked up again. "I love John better than anyone else on earth. If I'd betrayed him, even without meaning to, I'd kill myself."

"You know, at home I've got myself involved in this sort of

thing occasionally. And I have found that I have never kept anything back from the police—not for long, anyway. But I've often had to fight them to accept my interpretation of the facts."

She gave him a long, considering look, then jumped up and stood beside her chair with hands clasped, like a schoolchild confessing to a teacher. "I wrote to John, as Chester advised me, telling him to come and see Josiah Ahlberg that night. Chester said he would talk to his brother, and persuade him to give John an interview. I didn't know whether John came or not. Till yesterday morning. As soon as I'd heard about Josiah, I put through a call to Pittsburgh and told him what had happened."

"What did he say?"

"He said he'd been to Mr. Ahlberg's office, but it was locked. A journey wasted. So he started hitchhiking back."

"What time was this interview supposed to take place?"

"Oh, I forgot. Chester told me later he'd fixed it with Josiah for 10:30 that night. So I rang John to tell him. . . . Oh, I'm so afraid! What am I to do, Nigel?"

"Ten-thirty? That was a curious time, wasn't it?"

"Oh, well, Mr. Ahlberg worked till all hours, Mark told me once."

"And John is now on the run, I suppose. You know, Sukie— we'll assume him innocent—he ought to come straight back here and give the police his evidence. They're bound to catch up with him sooner or later; he'll simply hurt himself by running away."

"But I don't know where he is now," she wailed. "And he's got hardly any money."

Nigel sighed heavily. "Did John ever talk to you about this plagiarism affair?"

"Of course." Her eyes flashed. "Ahlberg stole his ideas, and then had John sacked for putting them into his thesis. John told me once—" She broke off, her hand going to her mouth in the immemorial woman's gesture.

"Yes?"

"No, it's nothing."

"Don't keep things back, Sukie."

"Oh, very well," she said meekly. "He told me he'd like to break into Ahlberg's office and take away that snake's own article. But of course he couldn't. He wasn't allowed to come inside Cabot for a year."

"But he came last Thursday?"

"That was because Mr. Ahlberg had permitted one visit."

"How do you know?"

"I *told* you—Chester said his brother had given the okay. I figured Josiah would have obtained the Master's consent, if that's needed."

"Well, look, if John does get in touch with you, tell him to come back here, pronto. If he's innocent—"

"He *is!*"

"—he's just snarling up things for everyone."

"But you'll help me, Nigel?" Her gray eyes dwelt on his with imploring intensity.

"I'll do what I can."

"Oh, bless you!" The young woman seized his hand, kissed the back of it, and scooping up her bag, hurried from the room. . . .

And that is as may be, thought Nigel. Most women are good actresses in an emergency: some don't even need one. Sukie? Time will tell. She loves John "better than anyone else on earth." Better than Mark? I suspect so.

Nigel's pale-blue eyes held an expression of guilelessness; which had been misinterpreted by many and had been the downfall of some.

He bent his mind now to two queer ambiguities in the story Sukie had told. First, how very strange that Josiah Ahlberg should have agreed to an interview with an ex-pupil he had been instrumental in suspending. Whether he or John was the guilty party, an interview seemed equally unlikely. If Josiah had stolen John's ideas, he would hardly wish to talk it over with the young man; unless, of course, John had since found some lever, some way to blackmail his tutor. And if John had in fact committed plagiarism, why should Josiah be willing to see him again?

In any case, according to Sukie, it was not John who had begged for an interview, but Chester who had arranged it. Why? And how? Did he have so much influence with Josiah? Was he so eager to do a service to the boy's sister, with whom he was no longer on intimate terms—if ever he had been? Or could it be to get back into her good graces and supplant Mark who had supplanted him? It did seem out of character—with what one knew about Chester.

And, then, the timetable. If Josiah was shot at 10:08 or thereabouts, under cover of the Food Man's shouts, and *if* Mark and John were both telling the truth when they said they'd arrived at Josiah's office, at 10:15 and 10:30 respectively, and *if* some third person had shot Josiah, and arranged for the other two to turn up shortly afterward and smear themselves with suspicion—no, too many indeterminate ifs.

The body having been removed to the locker room seemed to point a finger at John: he'd be the one who needed to gain time, to get as far away as possible from the scene of the crime, to establish an alibi maybe. But John was still in Pittsburgh when Sukie rang him yesterday. Surely a guilty man would not have gone straight back to his last known address? Well, he could suppose he was safe there till the body was found; and he had to husband his money. And, if John or any other member of the House was the killer, what advantage was it to defer the finding of the body, particularly when carrying it down to the basement must have involved great risk?

There was one permutation, Nigel reflected, which would

ravel things up even worse. A shot Josiah and left him in the room: B or C (Mark or John) did *not* find the door locked, went in, discovered the corpse, and losing his head, carted Josiah down to the locker room: out of sight, out of mind. A man who could later be *proved* to have had an appointment with Josiah for that night could conceivably have lost his head thus. Mark destroyed the note from Josiah, said nothing to the police, and possibly would never have done so but that a student had spotted him leaving B entry.

All this was spinning theories out of thin air, as Nigel well knew. He spun another one: let A be Chester. He writes a note on Josiah's typewriter, signs it with Josiah's initials, puts it in Mark's mailbox: that gets one suspect on to the scene. He *says* to Sukie that he's fixed the interview with Josiah—untrue, but it gets suspect C on to the scene (loathing Josh as she did, Sukie would be most unlikely to verify with him that he is giving her brother an interview). Chester then flies off to London, and with a well-aimed shot from a space gun drills a hole in Josiah's skull at the range of several thousand miles.

That of course is not on. But how do we know that Chester *did* fly to London on the night before the crime?

5 ☞ "Only the Soldered Mouth Can Tell"

An answer to one of Nigel's questions was furnished that same evening. Risking dinner in Hall (a risk he at once regretted), he met Chester and Mark on their way out.

"So you're back. I must tell you how deeply sorry I am about your brother's death." It was the sort of thing one said to Chester quite compulsively.

"I appreciate your expression of sympathy. It's a great loss to us and to Cabot. A shocking loss."

"Shocking indeed. I wondered if you and Mark would come and have a drink with me later. Ten o'clock, say." . . .

Equipped with liquor—Nigel was sure it was far from being Mark's first drink of the evening—the brothers sat side by side on the green sofa. Chester looked a bit heavy-eyed still, his features taut and pale.

"I'm afraid you must have had to cut short your stay in Britain," Nigel suggested.

"Well, no, fortunately not. We'd finished our conferences: just a little private business to clear up, and that can be done by correspondence. Right now we have to make arrangements for the interment."

"A painful task."

Chester bowed his head.

"I hope father will get here in time. I've reached him at last," said Mark.

"It would be an ordeal for him at his age."

"So it will, Chester. Seeing the apple of one's eye shoveled into the earth."

Chester gave his brother a shocked look. "The ceremony will be more dignified than that. I've no doubt the President of Cabot will attend, and the Heads of Faculties."

"Big deal. That will be a great consolation to Josh."

"Now don't be bitter, Mark. It won't get us any place."

Mark shrugged, giving his brother a satirical look. In his dark, neat suit, his face somber, Chester possessed an authority, or at any rate a decisiveness, which Nigel had not felt till now.

"Have you any theories about who could have done this dreadful thing?" he asked Nigel. "Mark tells me you have some previous experience in criminal investigation."

Nigel smiled faintly: it was amusing to be treated like a junior executive interviewed for a post.

"I leave the theorizing to Lieutenant Brady. Have you met him yet?"

"Old Ches has had a real workout with him," said Mark in a dégagé manner. "Brady's been barking up Chester's alibi. Well, you don't have to look so stuffy. I kept him off you till you'd had your sleep out, didn't I, Ches?"

"Yes, yes. But I don't like this talk about alibis."

"I'd have thought you would. You weren't in—what do they call it?—the vicinity of the crime, as I was. And how! Or did Brady suspect you'd arranged for your Doppelgänger to stop over in Britain while you perpetrated the—"

"Can't you ever be serious, Mark? Naturally, Brady had to check up on my movements in Britain. He'll find they tally with my statement."

"Well," said Mark after a pause, "it's not a deadly secret between you and Brady, is it? Restate your statement, for Nigel's benefit."

"Why not? I didn't know you'd be interested. I flew over last Wednesday night, went straight to the airport hotel, where I'd engaged a room, and slept round the clock. I'm not so good on air travel, Nigel—can't get to sleep in the damned things—so I take a strong sedative after a flight and put up the 'Do not disturb' notice on my door. My first conference was not till the Friday afternoon, so I'd plenty of time to get in shape again. We had conferences over the weekend, through Monday. They're all down in my diary, together with the names and addresses of the organizers: Brady is checking on them as a formality. Early Tuesday I got this call from Mark."

"And were you in a tizzy!" offered Mark, his voice beginning to slur. "Why hadn't I got in touch with you sooner! Good God, man, we'd had Brady round our necks for hours after midnight. You're not the only one who needs sleep."

"I realize that. I didn't realize that at the time."

Mark, who had been helping himself freely to bourbon, spilled some on his tie and began dabbing at it with a silk handkerchief. He looked up owlishly at Nigel. "Crack that alibi if you can! What're you smiling at? When private eyes are smiling, the crocodiles weep no tears. What is your stance toward crocodiles, Nigel? Myself, I like them in alligator bags. And when I'm a rich man, Sukie, dear Sukie, shall have an alligator bag."

"You'd better go to bed," said Chester repressively.

"I guess I better had—had better, if you prefer it." Mark rose uncertainly to his feet. "Poor old Josh. 'That short potential stir/That each can make but once' . . . He's made it. What is he now—a meek member of the resurrection?—who knows? Good night, Nigel, and good night, Chester, and good night, ladies. 'How many times these low feet staggered/Only the soldered mouth can tell.' We all come to it."

Mark lurched to the door: they heard his feet staggering down the stone staircase. Chester glanced apologetically at Nigel. "He feels this more than he cares to admit."

Going to the window, Nigel let up the shade and looked out. A new moon showed Mark tacking across the court.

"Let's take a stroll down to the river. It's a lovely night. If you're not too tired."

"Suits me."

They walked along a street of elegant frame houses, gleaming chalkily in the moonshine, and turned left. The Cabot bridge was a few hundred yards ahead. A jalopy, boys and girls perched all over it like birds in an aviary, sped past them.

"You need to be careful along the river at night. There've been some muggings recently," said Chester nervously.

"I wanted to ask you something without Mark present. Did he have bad trouble with Josiah?"

Chester's tone was stiff. "I don't know that I care to enter into that subject."

"You understand, don't you, that Mark could be in a bit of a jam? If I'm to help him—and Sukie—I need to anticipate the sort of things the police might bring up against him."

Chester was silent for a few moments. "Well, if it's not telling tales out of school . . . Josh was a bit hard on him—on us both, I guess. After our mother died, when Mark and I were in our teens, father was away a great deal of the time; and Josh behaved as if he were in loco parentis. He disciplined us some, and Mark wasn't the kind to lie down under that. So, when he found he was cutting no ice with Mark, Josh—I shouldn't be saying this—but he did some talebearing to father. I'm afraid he could be very, very mean in those days. It was just boyish escapades on Mark's part—I don't want to create a wrong impression: he was a bit frisky, nothing more."

"But your father threatened to cut him out of his will, didn't he?"

"How in the world d'you know that?"

"People gossip in these academic communities."

They were leaning over the parapet of the Cabot bridge, the water splintering into jags of light beneath them, the university boathouse a dark hump against the skyline on their left.

"Funny you should mention it here. When he was a senior, Mark beat up a man and flung him over this bridge."

"Out of high spirits?"

"Oh, nothing like that, believe me," Chester solemnly replied. "This man was a drug peddler; sold heroin and pot to students— you know, marihuana."

"Our old friend, Marihuana of the Moated Grange."

Chester laughed politely. "Mark said this man had gravely damaged a friend of his—given him an addiction."

"Well, it seems a commendable action on Mark's part, then."

"Father didn't take it like that. You see, the man threatened to make a public scandal of it. He said Mark was one of his— well, clients. I guess it was a piece of blackmail—he'd known father was a rich man and thought he'd pay up to avoid the drug scandal."

"And did he?"

"You don't know father! No, but he was furious with Mark for taking the action he did. He tried to keep the incident out of the press, but some tabloid gossip writer got hold of the story and went to town on it."

"I see. And did Josiah come into this?"

Chester held back his answer, then said slowly, "I don't have any firsthand knowledge—I wasn't brought in on the family discussions. But Mark did tell me later that Josh took a very antagonistic view, in fact that he credited the drug peddler's story rather than Mark's."

"And passed on his own conviction to your father?"

"He would do that. But I don't believe he persuaded father that Mark had ever taken drugs: it was Mark's violence that upset the old man. He heard Mark was a bit stoned when he beat up this man, and he'd had a traumatic experience himself which gave him a somewhat warped point of view toward liquor."

"Yes?" said Nigel patiently.

"When his first wife was killed, father was driving the car, and it transpired he wasn't quite sober."

The water slurred and slurped against the piers of the bridge. A fitful wind rustled the sycamores along the bank.

"And what about you?"

"Me?"

"Did Josiah try to get you in bad with your father too?"

"I guess I was a more docile type than Mark. He couldn't stand for being disciplined, whereas I—well, I let the storms blow themselves out over my head. I am speaking of the period when we were adolescents, you'll appreciate. Frankly, father didn't give a row of beans for me at that time. And Josh couldn't see me as any sort of competitor, so he left me alone for the most part."

"Competitor for what?"

"Oh, I don't know. Dad's favor maybe," said Chester uncomfortably. "And Josh was an overly ambitious character."

Ambitious enough to steal a pupil's glory? Nigel wondered, but he did not broach that subject immediately.

As they strolled back to Hawthorne House, Nigel asked Chester if he had ever had a key to his brother's office.

"No. I don't quite understand what you mean though."

"Each room has a spare key, which is kept in the Superintendent's room?"

"That is so."

"If Josiah was expecting a visitor, would he usually push the catch on the lock, so that the chap could walk in?"

"Sometimes maybe. I'd say not as a general rule."

"He seems to have been expecting two people that night."

"Two?"

"Mark was one."

"Oh, sure. John Tate. It had slipped my memory."

"How did you manage to make him agree to giving Tate an interview?"

Chester's face—he was passing under a street lamp—looked confused. He stumbled on the uneven sidewalk, and recovered himself after gripping Nigel's arm.

"Oh, Sukie talked me into doing it. I'm not too happy about my share in the—well, it wasn't exactly deception, but I did suggest to Josiah that John had latterly been feeling contrite about the affair and wanted to work his passage back to Hawthorne, and was hoping Josh could give him some assignment in the meantime."

"How did your brother react to this?"

"He agreed, though he was pretty grudging about it."

"Rather surprising that he agreed at all, wasn't it?"

"It certainly surprised me. You know, what has occurred to me since is that Josh may have suspected John had found some fresh piece of evidence against him, and he just had to find out from the boy what it might be."

"So you believe your brother was the villain of the plagiarism scandal?"

"No, no, I did *not* say that," Chester protested.

"His death is not on your conscience?"

"Now, just a moment! I will not permit you to talk that way! I—"

"But you arranged the interview with the man who may well be his murderer."

Chester's indignation collapsed. He gave a shaky little deprecatory laugh. "Well, frankly, Nigel, I won't say that's not occurred to me once or twice. But I refuse to credit that Sukie's brother would do such a thing."

"Not to a man who's ruined his career at the start?"

"His career's not been ruined, only checked. He's not the type to— I'd as soon believe Mark had done such a dreadful thing."

"Well," said Nigel flatly, "Mark seems to be the other most likely candidate." . . .

Dressing the next morning, Nigel let his mind run over the conversations of the night before. Surprisingly, it did seem that Mark was reacting more strongly than Chester to their brother's death; of course it might be because he'd had more to drink, but Nigel doubted this. Chester, though he'd unbuttoned quite a bit during their walk, had kept himself, unlike Mark, under control. He had been evasive over one or two points; and there was something brittle about him—he seemed to carry his personality with gingerly caution, as if it were a priceless vase, but one could understand this in a man who had a mild persecution mania and was accident-prone. Mark was the wild one, something of an escapist. Emotionally immature (as no doubt the censorious Josiah had dinned into him often enough), but with a good crop of emotion waiting to mature. Of the three, Josiah was the real enigma. Ambitious, his father's favorite, fidgety, sardonic, bossy to his brothers, uninterested in women, but surely no homosexual, a heavy pipe smoker—the things Nigel knew about him did not add up to a coherent character. And he could gain no more firsthand evidence now: which was a nuisance, because the character of a murdered man may lead one to the identity of his murderer.

What was it, for example, that had made Josiah go talebearing to his father (if he did) or to show hostility to Mark (if he had) over the drug-traffic episode? Personal dislike? A sense of responsibility as the eldest son? Pure malice? Why, after all, should a man who was already the apple of his father's eye put in overtime courting his father's favor? . . .

As Nigel approached the dining hall, he saw a group of students clustered round the partition which divided it from the lobby. Elections for the Student Council were soon to take place, and upon this wall were pinned what might be called the campaign manifestoes of the various candidates, some earnest, some fairly frivolous.

The young men politely made way for Nigel, giving him good morning, covertly watching his face while he moved up to the wall.

Dead center was an item which certainly had not been there yesterday—a large and eye-catching montage. It was a photograph of Chester Ahlberg, blown up from a House group, and wearing an anxious expression. Across his knees had been superimposed a cutout apparently from *Playboy*—a totally naked redhead sprawled in a totally abandoned fashion, pushing up her enormous breasts at Chester as if inviting him to eat them. Beneath, in black-crayon capitals, ran the legend:

VOTE FOR ME! I STAND FOR FREE ELECTIONS, FREE THOUGHT AND FREE LOVE.

"Well, well," said Nigel, wondering whether it did not go beyond the latitude allowed in this democratic House. The students around him did seem more shocked than amused, though one said, "I didn't know Ahlberg was running in the election," and another muttered, "I guess he's standing, anyway."

Finally a graduate broke through the group, uttered an exclamation of disgust, tore the exhibit from the wall, and walked off with it.

"The Church Militant."

"Cyrus is the president of the Baptist Union in Cabot," someone explained to Nigel.

"It's none of my business, but does anyone know who did this poster?" asked Nigel, when some of the group were sitting at breakfast with him.

It seemed that none of them did.

"Chester Ahlberg's not that unpopular in the House, surely?"

"No, Mr. Strangeways," said a pink-faced youth. "But someone sure must have it in for him."

"It's happened before—this sort of nonsense?"

"Yeah. One day early in the semester, I was opening my mailbox—I live in Chester's entry—and he stopped by to open his. He put his hand in, and—well, he put it on something real ugly." The youth paused, blushing.

"A turd," said a hardier friend.

"And it was never discovered who—?"

"Nope."

"Well, it must have been someone who knew Mr. Ahlberg's combination. But that didn't get the Senior Tutor any place," another boy explained.

Each member of the House had a mailbox, which was opened by turning a dual pointer above it to a certain combination of figures, like a safe.

So it looks as if Chester was right, thought Nigel; he doesn't have persecution mania, he's persecuted. And in a particularly disagreeable way.

After breakfast he found the Master in his study, with the offensive poster lying on the desk in front of him. "Will you take a look at this."

"I've seen it, Zeke."

"One of our religious firebrands came tearing in just now. Protested it let down the tone of the House, was an example of my overly permissive regime. Maybe it is." The Master gave one of his skull-like grins. "An interesting idea," he said, glancing at the montage, "though I doubt if redheads come within Chester's field of concentration. Well, it'll give the Senior Tutor something to exercise his deductive intelligence upon."

"Like the Thing in the Mailbox?" Nigel asked.

"Ah-ha! So you're beginning to concern yourself with our problems, Nigel. I knew you'd not be able to keep away from them for long."

"Zeke, if Josiah consented to give John Tate an interview here, would he have to ask your permisison first?"

"Theoretically, yes. In the case of any student who has been suspended. In practice, he probably wouldn't: he was a law unto himself, was Josiah, poor fellow. But what—?"

"He apparently did agree to see him the night of his death."

"Oh, my Lord!"

"Josiah never mentioned it to you?"

"He certainly did not."

"If he had, what would have been your attitude?"

"I'd have advised him to make sure he had a witness present," the Master said.

"To prevent violence?"

"No. Not that really. John is the type who blusters, but if you call his bluff, he climbs down."

"But he didn't climb down after accusing Josiah of stealing his ideas. Which suggests it was not bluff that time."

The Master uncoiled from his chair, went to the French window, and stood looking out, his back to Nigel.

"I know. That occurred to me quite a while ago. It lies heavy on my mind—the idea that we may have done John a grievous wrong. But at the time, Nigel, well, it was unthinkable that a Cabot professor could—"

There was a knock on the door, and Lieutenant Brady entered.

"Have you come to make a progress report?" Zeke asked pleasantly.

"A no-progress report would be more accurate, Mr. Edwardes. We've combed every room here for the murder weapon, without result."

"Which suggests that the murderer came from outside?"

"I'm afraid not. The killer had several days to dispose of it. We're using the latest equipment to find if he tossed it into the river. But there's several million other places in this city he could have stashed it away. We have a call out for John Tate: we rang his Pittsburgh address, but the landlady says he's not been there since the day before the murder. I've contacted the top brass at your Scotland Yard, Mr. Strangeways; they're checking Mr. Chester Ahlberg's statement. I've also checked up on you, and they told me quite a piece. I should be happy to have your cooperation."

Oh *my,* thought Nigel. He said, "Good of you—and I'd be interested to see something of your methods over here, but I'm kept pretty busy on my research—"

"You get anywhere with Miss Tate yesterday morning?" Brady asked.

"My goodness, Lieutenant, you're quick on the ball!"

"My pop used to say, 'If you don't hustle, you'll sink.' You were going to tell me about Miss Tate."

"Was I? Well, it seems she arranged through Chester for her brother to have an interview with Professor Ahlberg. At 10:30 P.M. on the night of Thursday last. She telephoned to John, saying this interview had been arranged. She did not see him herself. That is her story."

"Period. I get you. So that young woman's going to be pretty upset when next I see her." Brady's green eyes dwelled piercingly upon Nigel's. "Does she figure she's going to hire you to keep her brother out of the clutches of the brutal police?"

Nigel grinned. "No salary was mentioned."

"I'd watch out for that one. They're Reds, the whole family, and she's the worst of them."

Nigel did not attempt to play that ball. Brady sent down a more direct one. "You've been some time coming through with this information about John Tate's interview, Mr. Strangeways."

"You've had it now. You were already looking for Tate, and the information would not have expedited your finding him."

"If you boys are going to get mad with each other, I'll take my work to another room," said Zeke, smiling amiably.

"No, I want a word with May," Nigel said.

"She's somewhere around. Try the drawing room."

"I'll be keeping in touch, Lieutenant."

"See you."

With the expression of a dog from whom a large bone has removed itself, Brady watched Nigel walk out.

May Edwardes was writing letters at her desk. "The secret of getting American stamps to stick on envelopes is not to lick them too much. When I first got here I found it impossible. It took me a year and a great expense of saliva to learn how to do it properly." May turned toward him in her chair. "You're needing something?"

"I want you to talk to me about John Tate. How well did you know him?"

"Well, now, Nigel, I'm not a motherly person, as you may have noticed. He didn't come to me with his troubles. But I found him interesting to talk with. Considerable maturity on the surface, but if you probed much you found yourself breaking through—as with most of these young men—to a gulf of naïveté."

"Is he what Brady calls a Red?"

"A Red? Oh, I don't know. He's concerned politically. He's rather a radical. I know Zeke had to speak to him about some of his activities as secretary for the May the Second Committee."

"How did he take that?"

"I saw him coming out of the study. He looked like a child who's been corrected. Terribly down-in-the-mouth. Bewildered."

"Bark worse than bite?"

"He does tend to cave in when he meets opposition. Mind you, Zeke can be very formidable. I'd say John has the same quixotic urges as his sister, but less stamina."

"What about his family?"

"The parents divorced some years ago. I don't think John saw much of his mother after that. Sukie's been sister and mother to him: they're awfully close."

"Ever meet their father?"

"Let me see—yes, I did once. Of course one's heard about him. Not a very well-balanced man, I should think. I gather he has great intelligence, but probably like all these Hollywood people, he lives half the time in a fantasy world. Or I guess he did till he had that McCarthy trouble."

"It ruined his career?" Nigel asked.

"Well, I imagine it damaged it. You know he recanted—ran for the nearest burrow, you might say. There was a story that he informed against some of his liberal friends too."

"Which wouldn't improve his relationship with two crusading children."

"No. But the young are very hard on everyone's failings but their own." May gave Nigel a very straight look. "Are the police after John?"

"Yes. Tell me, May, do you think it *was* plagiarism on his part, or was Josiah the real culprit?"

May Edwardes twisted the rings on her bony fingers. "I wish I knew. I've never been able to make up my mind. And I certainly wish we knew where he is now."

"I think you've told me," said Nigel.

6 ☞ The Missing Plagiarist

Nigel went back to his room and rang Sukie's number. There was no reply. He was settling down to a book when a voice called to him from the courtyard below. He opened the window. Chester Ahlberg was there, looking distraught, with Charles Reilly.

"Did I drop my passport in your room last night?" Chester asked. "It's disappeared."

"I've not seen it. Come up and look, if you like."

Chester searched down the sides of sofa and armchairs, without result.

"I simply can't figure out where—"

"When did you last see it?"

"Well, I put it in my mackintosh pocket after I'd shown it at the airport. Didn't miss it till this morning. I've looked all over my rooms."

"What's the hurry?" said Charles. "You're not going to flee the country, are you?"

"But it's perfectly ridiculous, I never lose my passport."

"I daresay it dropped out of your pocket. The cabby will return it. Sure a passport's no good to anyone but its owner. You can always get another one, anyway."

"That's *not* the point, Charles—"

"Where else did you go after you returned?" Nigel interrupted.

"I carried my baggage up to my room," Chester said slowly.

"Then—what did I do next?—oh, yes, of course, I went round to see Mark. Let's ask him."

Mark had a pupil and was not best pleased by the incursion.

"Oh, go on, take the place to bits. First the police, now you," he said wearily. Chester was already darting about, feeling down the sides of chairs, peering under the desk, riffling the papers on a side table. This last action, Nigel noticed, laid bare the cover of a copy of *Playboy;* but Chester passed it over without comment, and hurried into the bedroom, Charles Reilly at his heels.

"What the hell does he want his goddam passport for?" grumbled Mark, and turned back to his pupil.

Nigel casually turned over the pages of *Playboy.* One page had been torn out. Nigel made a mental note of its number and the magazine date of issue. Presently Chester and Charles returned, empty-handed.

"Now don't get in such a lather," Charles was saying. "You'll find it eventually. Before you next take off. You Americans are always fretting to go somewhere you're not. This craze for globe-trotting. There's only the one passport worth having, and that's a passport to Paradise."

"I'm awfully sorry, Mark, to—"

"Really, Chester, if I'd found the darned thing I'd have told you. Now for the Lord's sake beat it. Haven't you any work to do?"

They went to Chester's room. Nigel, who had not been there before, found it the antithesis of Mark's—pernickety in its tidiness, the furniture placed like soldiers on parade, the books numbered off and dressed alphabetically from left to right, a bright fire burning. There were some admirable prints on the wall, and two examples of early nineteenth-century American masters.

"Do you suppose Josiah *had* a passport to Paradise?" Nigel asked idly as he ran his eye over the books. Chester was making coffee in the next room.

"He'd be lucky if he reached Purgatory, from all I've heard," Charles said finally.

"That's a nice Christian remark, Charles, I must say."

"It's the trut'."

"And more characteristic of you than corny stuff about passports to Paradise," Nigel murmured. As he turned away from a shelf filled with biographies of financiers and captains of industry he saw that Charles Reilly's florid face was darkly suffused.

"You damned blasé Englishmen wouldn't recognize the trut' if it poked you in the eye. I've a mind to do it, to prove my point."

Nigel shook his head. "Sorry. There's enough trouble in this House without two elderly gentlemen coming to fisticuffs. But did you have a *personal* grudge against Josiah?"

"I did not." Charles's tongue splayed out between his thick lips—a curious mannerism that took him when he was nervous or about to deliver himself of a malicious remark. But all he added was "I just didn't like the fella."

Nigel let it pass, though he was aware that he had touched a sensitive spot. Why should I start needling Charles? he wondered. . . .

Sukie was in when he rang her half an hour later. "May I come and see you, now?" he asked.

"Here?"

"Yes."

There was a brief pause. "Okay. Come to lunch. I'll fix you an omelet."

Sukie gave him directions for finding her apartment. She had one floor of a shabby frame house in a run-down section of the town. Children, white and Negro, played on the sidewalk in front of it: empty cardboard containers were piled beside the door: damp stains disfigured the wall of the staircase. The sitting room presented the chaotic appearance of many students' apartments: books, pamphlets and cushions on the floor, the table hastily cleared for a meal, tattered curtains which had once been scarlet. In this shabby, slovenly nest, Sukie stood out with almost preternatural clarity of definition: a dark-blue jersey and fawn skirt set off the lines of her small, trim body; her face, for all the uncertain look on it, was vivid as a camellia. Artemis, he thought; no, Vergil's warrior maiden, Camilla.

"Have they found John?" was the first thing she said.

"Not yet."

"Oh, well— Would you like some Dubonnet?"

"That would be nice."

She took a sticky bottle and two glasses from a cupboard. "It's gin and bitter lemon you really like, isn't it?" she said shyly. "But I hadn't time to buy any."

"How's Emily Dickinson going?"

"Can't you imagine?"

Nigel sipped his drink. His pale-blue eyes rested upon her without guile or pressure. "I do wish, Sukie, you could have told me the truth."

"But I—"

"No, no, my dear, don't make it worse. You told me you rang John at Pittsburgh as soon as you heard about Josiah's death," said Nigel gently. "You told me he answered you and described how he'd come to Josiah's office and found it locked."

"Yes, and so he did."

"So he did, maybe. But you never spoke with him on the telephone. Brady rang his landlady in Pittsburgh and she said he had not been in the house since that Thursday."

Sukie's black lashes veiled her eyes. "I rang his place of work, not his house."

"He hadn't been there either."

Her face crumpled. "I thought you were on my side," she wailed childishly.

"So I am. But what can I do if you won't tell me the truth?"

"I'm sorry, Nigel, but I knew you'd pass on to Brady what I told you. I hoped it would send the cops on—on a false trail."

"My poor child! Do stop playing cops and robbers. It simply isn't your game. The police have your photograph of him: they're bound to catch up with him before long. I told you the right thing for him to do was—"

"He's got a beard in the photo. He shaved it off," she began triumphantly.

"So he could get into Hawthorne without being recognized."

"I never—"

"Oh, Sukie, for an intelligent girl who acts like a half-wit, you take the cake. Don't you suppose Brady'll have the beard brushed off some of the copies of the photo he sends round?"

"Let them find him, that's all—let them find him!" cried Sukie defiantly.

"Where is he?"

The gray eyes looked into Nigel's with an expression of the purest innocence. "How should I know?"

Nigel sighed. "All right. You'd better go and fix us omelets. . . . And don't forget to make one for John too," he added as Sukie reached the door.

She spun round. "I— *What* was that again?"

"John had better eat with us. It's time I talked to him."

"Are you out of your mind?"

"He's here. I know it. In this house." Nigel caught a momentary flick of her eyes upward. "On the top floor."

"You're crazy, Nigel. What's come over you?"

"Now look, Sukie. John goes to Hawthorne and gets a dreadful shock. He finds Josiah—dead, I hope. He panics. Hides the body to gain himself time. Then the reaction comes. I gather that when John is faced with a sudden crisis he tends to lose his nerve —runs for the nearest burrow," said Nigel, freely drawing upon

May Edwardes' observations. "Runs to mother—you're his mother as well as his sister, my dear Sukie. He coughs it all up in mother's lap," Nigel went on with intentional crudeness. "So here he is—and here *you* are, compounding a felony or whatever it's called in this country."

Sukie was gazing at him spellbound, like a child listening to a fairy tale, her fists clenched and the pretty breasts rising and falling rapidly under her sweater.

"You—how can you know?—it isn't true, it isn't true!" Her voice had slurred up an octave. She gripped the edge of the door as if without its support she would collapse.

"You've done enough for him," said Nigel equably. "Now let me try. Go and fetch him. If you don't, I will."

By now the girl had no resistance left. She withdrew, presumably to fetch her elusive brother. Or maybe she was telling him to beat it before Nigel sent for Brady. Nigel contemplated the risk with equanimity. There was also the risk that, since he was the only person who knew of John's whereabouts, this rather unreliable young man might dash in and silence him with a revolver. Minutes passed—five, ten. Nigel began to fear he had misjudged. Then the door opened and Sukie entered, hand in hand with a young Negro.

"This is my brother," she announced rather breathlessly.

"I'm happy to know you, Mr. Strangeways."

"I very much doubt it, but still—" said Nigel, shaking hands. "Now, Sukie, what about those omelets? And no tomato for me—I can't abide the vegetable. While you're fixing them, John might go and wash that stuff off his face."

"We thought it a good—"

"*Please,* Sukie dear, spare me the story of your brilliant devices for outwitting the police," interrupted Nigel, succumbing (as he frequently did) to the temptation to show off. "You've been hiding your brother with a Negro family upstairs, who are devoted to you because of your work for desegregation. You blacked his face and hands in case the police should come poking about in your friends' apartment. Silly girl. What I could see through in five seconds, Brady would in three—or maybe ten."

"I *told* you, John," said Sukie. "He's the Wizard of Oz. He ought to be suppressed. It's those hypnotic X-ray eyes."

"*I'm hungry,*" Nigel roared.

But he was deadly serious when half an hour later, the meal over and coffee before them, he faced brother and sister.

"Now I want you to tell me *everything* that happened the night you visited Josiah Ahlberg."

John glanced at Sukie; his intelligent brown eyes still had traces under them of whatever he had used to make up as a Negro. The small jaw was quite firm, but the eyes tended to shift away from the person he was talking to: simple nervousness, Nigel wondered, or natural shiftiness? It was, inevitably, an immature face. And here John was, silently appealing to his sister for direction. She was leaning back, collapsed in her chair like a frowning pretty doll.

John turned to Nigel. "I don't see why you should believe me," he muttered.

"I've an open mind."

Sukie gave an overwrought sigh. "And then you'll hand him over to Brady."

"No. He'll hand himself over."

"Thus establishing my innocence. Like in a suspense novel," remarked John truly.

Sukie reached out a hand and gripped his. "Go on, sweetie. Get it over with."

She held John's hand all through the narration which, supplemented by a few answers to questions from Nigel, ran as follows:

He had entered Hawthorne House by the main gateway that

night, choosing a moment when he could see the man in the lighted lodge turn his back to take a telephone call. He had met no one in the courtyard on his way to Josiah's office. He arrived there perhaps a minute or two after 10:30, the time of the appointment. He knocked, but there was no answer, which made him wonder if Josiah, notoriously fussy about punctuality, had already left. Knocking again, he turned the handle: the door was not locked. John went in, and found his ex-tutor lying on the floor beside his desk, with a hole in his temple.

"Did you touch him then?"

"Not immediately, sir. I—I was sort of stunned."

John's first impulse was to beat it fast. He tried to remember if he had left fingerprints on anything except the outside door-knob. Panic began to close round him. Here he was, with the corpse of a man everyone knew he had cause to hate. He made a strong effort to keep the panic at bay. All he could think of was how to buy himself time—time to get far away from this hideous room.

"You never thought to give the alarm?" Nigel interrupted.

"Well, I ask you!"

"But you'd not brought a revolver with you?"

"I certainly had not," the boy heatedly replied.

"If you'd rung for help from the office, they'd have found you with a dead man but no gun you could have shot him with. You'd have been cleared. They'd have searched the ground beneath the window. No gun there."

"Okay, okay, I guess you're right. But my brain probably wasn't in working order," said John ruefully.

Then he remembered the locker room. It was near Josiah's entrance, in the basement, and never used now. He bent to lift up the dead man, noticed bloodstains on the wooden floor beneath his head, put Josiah down again, pulled a mat over the stains, examined desk and chair for other stains, and found none. He opened the door cautiously. All was quiet outside.

He humped the body again—it was dreadfully heavy for so small a man—released the door catch so it would lock behind him, and was about to leave when it occurred to him that Josiah might well have recorded his appointment with John in a diary or memorandum book.

So he laid the body down a second time and began to examine Josiah's desk. There was an office diary there, but no record of the appointment—nor, at a cursory glance, on any of the other papers lying around. John even steeled himself to take Josiah's private diary from a jacket pocket. No appointment there.

"I realized I was just putting off the moment when I'd have to carry him from the first floor, past other people's doors, down the steps to the basement."

Nigel still had to remind himself that the first floor in the States was the ground floor in Britain.

"So at last I carried him through the door and downstairs. I was very lucky. The locker room was open. I hadn't thought of that. Then I pushed the body into a locker—that was awful—and clicked the door shut."

"Was he stiff?"

"Stiff? No. No, he wasn't stiff. But he was still warm. That unnerved me. I thought all dead bodies got cold at once. His hand swung against my face as I lifted him in. It was awful. I thought perhaps he wasn't dead after all." The boy's mouth began to quiver. "He *was* dead, sir, wasn't he?"

"Oh, yes. The shot would have killed him instantly."

John had stood in the dark, not daring to switch on any lights. His relief at having smuggled the corpse away unobserved was giving way to a paralyzed mental despair. He recalled—what he had quite forgotten in the horror of his discovery and its aftermath—that Josiah's brother knew about the appointment. Sukie had told him over the long-distance telephone that Chester would be in London on the day of it: but he would return early the next week. By hiding the body, John had bought himself only a few days. He must get away from Pittsburgh, to which he could so easily be traced once the alarm was given. He would go far west: but he hadn't enough money for the journey.

"So you went to Sukie?"

"Honest, I didn't want to get her into trouble. I just wanted the loan of some money. I never meant to—"

"It's all right, sweetie." Sukie turned her candid gray eyes on Nigel. "John was all in—all upset—when he arrived here. I just couldn't let him leave when he told me what had happened. It was *my* idea that he should hide out here for a while. He didn't want to."

Crusading again, thought Nigel.

Sukie went on: "I thought the cops would never look for him here—not upstairs among our Negro friends. And they didn't." She returned Nigel's sardonic look rather shamefacedly. "I know what you're thinking. I'm liable to have got *them* into trouble."

"They knew it was John when they agreed to shelter him?"

"Yes," she whispered, eyes downcast. "I didn't tell them the real truth, though. I made up a story about John's having to hide for a few days because—"

"Do you believe me?" John burst out. "D'you believe what I told you?"

"It's possible," Nigel returned coolly. "But you're a fearful pair for making up stories."

"Now don't you go bullying my sister!" John stood up, fists clenched.

Nigel ignored him. "So now you'll have to make up another story—to guard your Negro friends from being arrested as accessories. And it'd better be good."

There was a long silence in the tawdry little room. At last Sukie said, "What do you plan to do? Tell the police?"

"No. John's going to do that."

"You're deserting us!" Her eyes flashed.

"My dear child, it's John's best hope. Don't you see? John must tell Brady he'd been wandering about in a state of shock since the discovery. He's forgotten—repeat, forgotten—what happened to him in the interim. This morning he picks up a paper and reads that the police are looking for him. So he goes straight to the precinct and describes everything that happened, from the moment he entered Hawthorne House that night to the moment he left."

"You're crazy," muttered Sukie.

"No, he's not," said John. "That would stop you and the family upstairs getting mixed up in the thing at all."

"No, I won't have it. They'll beat you up at the station house. Till they find out where you've really been. You'd *never* get away with saying you lost your memory."

"Now take it easy, sis. I'm not getting you in any more trouble, see? They'll be much more interested in what I have to tell them about finding the body than in trying to trace my movements afterwards." Some of Sukie's steel was evident now in John's determined mien.

"*Must* he go now?" she asked Nigel.

"The sooner the better. But he must prepare his script first— in what paper did you read about the crime? haven't you any recollection of where you've been sleeping and eating?—that sort of thing, because they'll ask you."

"Let's see, the Negro quarter in the city," John promptly supplied. "It's all pretty hazy, I guess: but—well, I remember taking a bus ride out into the country one day and wandering round in the woods. And, yes—"

"Keep it for Brady. Or get Sukie to test out these interesting fictions, if you like. I must be off." Nigel gazed directly at the young man. "And don't let her persuade you into any more disappearing acts. I'm gambling on you, remember."

And that's about the wildest gamble I've ever made, thought Nigel, striding along an hour later between the river and the humming traffic. John appeared to be honest; but, if he possessed any of his sister's talent for misleading, Nigel would certainly lose. What he had gambled on was John's evident desire to keep Sukie out of trouble; but had John the moral stamina to go through with the plan, and not make another break for freedom?

His story of discovering the body had rung true enough, confirming Nigel's previous hunch that it had been hidden to buy someone a respite. And, if John was telling the truth about the time he'd arrived at the office, he was unlikely to have been the murderer: a gunshot would surely have been heard by someone at that hour of the night. His successful attempt to enter the House unobserved had rebounded on him in a way he could not have foreseen—if he was innocent.

John had said that the body was still warm when he touched it. This detail, as he had described it, carried a genuine conviction; and, a dead body's temperature falling one degree an hour on the average of time taken to fall to the temperature of the surrounding medium—in this case, a small, centrally heated room—did not conflict with the hypothesis that Josiah had been shot during the Food Man's clamor, roughly half an hour before John claimed to have discovered him. If he *had* killed Josiah, he was surely intelligent enough to have said the body was cold when he found it.

Nigel's long-odds gamble proved a winner, though, when the Master rang that evening to ask him over for a drink.

"Brady's just telephoned me," said Zeke. "He's on his way here. John Tate has given himself up."

7 ☞ The Concupiscent Poet

The Master and his wife were talking over drinks with Chester Ahlberg when Nigel arrived.

"But doesn't that prove young Tate is innocent?" Chester was saying strongly.

"Ah, here you are, Nigel. May I pour you some bourbon?" asked Zeke.

"Thanks. Good evening, May. Hello, Chester."

"It'll clear the air anyway," said May. "I feel I've been walking about in a thick fog these last days."

"You like ice, don't you, Nigel? Adapted yourself fast to our barbarous American habits."

"It's self-evident," Chester pursued. "No guilty man gives himself up to the police of his own free will." The Business School tutor's usual pompousness was laced with an almost aggressive sincerity.

"I only had a few words with Brady. He said nothing about John's having confessed—just that he walked into the precinct house this afternoon and made a statement," said Zeke urbanely.

"That boy's no murderer," May opined.

"I certainly *hope* not." Chester shook his head. "It would lie heavy on my conscience if I thought I'd encouraged an interview between poor Josh and—and the person who killed him."

"My dear Chester," said May, a trifle tartly, "there's no need to overburden us with your conscience as yet. I am much more

concerned with the treatment poor John may get at Police Headquarters. I gather their methods are notoriously crude."

"Now, now, May, my dear."

"But where's he been all this time?" asked Chester.

"The Lieutenant did not vouchsafe me that information. All
will be made plain in a few minutes. We must curb our curiosity
till then."

"Does Sukie know about this yet?" May asked.

"Brady said he'd spoken to her over the telephone," Chester
said.

"Very thoughtful of the man."

"She wanted to rush down at once, but he discouraged it.
She's been seeking the advice of a lawyer instead."

"I hate to think of her suffering under such terrible stress of
mind."

"Well, Chester," remarked May, who was for some reason at
her most formidable this evening, "let us divert our thoughts to
less painful matters. No doubt Mark is looking after her. Nigel,
you are very silent: have you no contribution to make to our
symposium?"

Looking noncommittally down his nose, Nigel, who seldom lost
an opportunity for introducing a cat into a pigeon loft, said, "I
was thinking how disinterested Chester is."

The person named gave him a wary glance. "I don't quite
follow you there."

"In rejecting the notion that John Tate is guilty."

"Well, of course he's not."

"Because, if he isn't, it has to be Mark. Hasn't it? Or is there
some other candidate I haven't heard of?"

The Master looked shaken; his wife raised her eyebrows.
Chester took some time to reply; but then he often did, as if he
had to shape a sentence in his mind before entrusting it to his
tongue. "Now that is a suggestion no sane person could accept

for an instant," he said firmly. "I am astonished to hear you make it. You surely cannot believe that Mark, my own brother—"

"I don't *believe* anything. I merely ask, if it wasn't John or Mark, who was it? Who else had motive and opportunity?"

"It's a very, very offensive suggestion." Chester was beginning to wind himself up. "I don't think you should bring such charges without Mark's being present."

"They're not charges," said Nigel wearily. "But if you prefer to stick your head in the sand, that's your affair."

"But, Nigel," Zeke objected, "what conceivable motive could Mark have?"

"He comes in for a share of Josiah's prospects." Nigel was tempted, and fell instantly. "Then there's only Chester between him and the father's fortune. You'd better watch out, Chester my boy."

"I consider your remarks to be in the worst possible taste," Chester replied heatedly.

"This symposium," remarked May, "should not degenerate into a Borgia supper."

"If this is by way of being a specimen of your humor—" Chester was cut off by a loud ring on the bell.

"That'll be Brady," said the Master, going out to open the door. When he returned, he beckoned to Nigel. "The Lieutenant would like a word with both of us. We'll go to the study."

Now I'm for it, thought Nigel. But Brady, sitting square and solid on a hard chair, flipped a hand at him amiably enough, refused a drink, and got down to business.

"We're holding John Tate."

"On what charge?" asked Zeke.

"You'll know when I tell you his statement. I'm afraid Mr. Strangeways will have to hear it again."

This sighting shot was unexpected, but not too hard to steer away from. "*Again?* What's all this?"

Brady's piercing green eyes flicked onto Nigel. "As the guy came to us only today, I figured he must have had some good advice recently."

"It's the advice I certainly would have given him if I'd had the opportunity," Nigel equivocally replied.

"Well, isn't that nice! So where did you find him, to give him this good advice you'd have given him if you'd found him?"

"Your dialectic has me groggy, Lieutenant. Is it your devious way of breaking it to me that John says *I* found him?"

"Well, that'll keep."

"No, it won't. Does he?"

"He does not." Brady gave Nigel a hard smile. "I guess he's been well coached."

"When you two have finished sparring, could we hear John's statement?" put in the Master.

Brady recounted it straight, without attempting to dig any more pitfalls for Nigel.

"Good God, the poor boy!" said Zeke. "What a horrible experience for him! So you're charging him with concealing information relevant to the crime?"

"That's the charge, as of now."

"But why *did* he wait all this time before coming to you?"

"He says he was in a state of shock. Only realized we wanted him when he picked up a paper this morning."

"What's he been doing in the meanwhile?"

"Wandering about in the city. Eating and sleeping in the Negro quarter. That's his story. It'd have given him plenty of time to hide the gun."

"He admits he took a gun to the interview?" asked Nigel.

"He's not all that crazy. And I'm not satisfied with this story of him spending days in a state of shock. I can't shake it yet. I'm getting a psychiatrist to work on him. That'll sort him out. My own belief is that someone was hiding him."

"Who?"

"His sister, could be."

"But I thought you'd searched her apartment," said Nigel.

"We did. She wouldn't hide him there, though." Brady gave Nigel a long, ruminative stare. "What d'you think of this story of his about discovering the body?"

"As you narrate it," replied Nigel smoothly, "it does sound quite plausible. Did you believe it?"

"I don't know. He sure had it pat. As though he'd tried it out on someone before. He remembers every detail, yet doesn't have more than a vague impression of his movements during the subsequent period. There's something wrong here. If only we could trace the purchase of a gun by him! Trouble over here, Mr. Strangeways, it's as easy to buy a gun as a sack of peanuts."

"By the way, you know Chester Ahlberg has lost his passport?"

"That stuffed shirt? No. Well, we'll keep an eye out for it. But it's father Ahlberg has me worried. Keeps ringing me, asking me why haven't I brought his son's murderer to justice, threatening to have my head if I don't solve the crime within a week. That old man's a heller, believe me."

"If anyone found a passport, he'd send it to the owner or hand it in somewhere, wouldn't he? It'd be no use to the finder."

"Normally, sure. But there's quite a trade in them. Substitute your own photograph. Forge the stamps over it. Delete the physical details chemically, and substitute your own. It's professional work, though. You telling me Chester Ahlberg has an expert forger lined up?"

"Not exactly. But it would have been possible for him to take the next plane back here, shoot his brother, fly to London again the same night, and turn up all present and correct at his first conference there next morning. Possible, with the time differences in the two countries."

Lieutenant Brady laughed shortly. "You kidding me, Mr. Strangeways? That's for the birds."

"You mean, obtain a phony passport with a false name, so that the airport people would have no record of a Chester Ahlberg flying in that night and flying out again?" asked the Master soberly.

"Something like that."

Brady laughed again. "So, why would he lose his *real* passport? It's the faked one he'd have to get rid of."

"Yes. That's just the trouble. Still, it might be worth inquiring from the international airlines at Charlton airport if a man answering his description came in from Britain that Thursday night."

"It's crazy," the Lieutenant protested. Then, with a hard look at Nigel, "You're trying to sidetrack me from your own client."

"John Tate's not my client. Will you have the inquiries made —if only to stop up that hole?"

"All right. I'll put someone onto it." Brady got up and stretched. "I must be on my way. Would you do one little thing for me?"

"Of course."

"I don't seem to get any place with Mark Ahlberg. Maybe you can. There's a discrepancy of evidence—"

"Yes. John Tate says he found the office door unlocked at 10:30. Mark said it was locked at 10:15."

"What it is to have brains! Good night. Be seeing you. Good night, Master." . . .

"One thing you and Sukie'll have in common."

"What's that?" asked Mark abruptly. He was sitting at his cluttered desk after dinner, studying a pupil's essay.

"Total chaos."

"Uh-huh. Be with you in a minute."

Nigel prowled quietly around the disordered room. Gramophone records lay on books which lay on papers which as often as not lay on the floor. He turned over the pile of journals on a

side table: the copy of *Playboy* was no longer there: he selected
an issue of the *Sewanee Review*.

It was difficult, he reflected, to get a grip on Mark. A good
English scholar who subscribed to *Playboy* and apparently had
no objection to its being seen that he did. A couldn't-care-less
character, who had come to blows with a drug peddler because
of a friend's downfall. A young man who had won a girl away
from his brother, yet seemed not to value his winnings overmuch.
Mark was something of an enigma: was this the natural outcome
of his personality or a deliberate covering up? If the latter, it
would be the most successful kind, which drapes itself in a quite
transparent manner, free and easy, innocent seeming, uncompli-
cated. Yet it was a far from negative personality: it persuaded
you into acceptance, compelled you into its own idiom.

"Well, that's that," Mark said, laying down the essay. "A
beautiful, ardent girl. And the sooner she becomes a wife and
mother, and abandons academic hopes, the happier we shall be."

He took bottles from a cupboard and poured drinks.

"How is she?" asked Nigel.

"Blooming, I've no doubt. Oh, you mean Sukie. She's in a
tizzy about John—imagines they've got him in a cellar, with elec-
trodes clamped on his foot."

"Where's he been all this time?"

"Either Sukie won't tell me, or she genuinely doesn't know."

"I'd have thought she'd confide in *you*."

Mark took a meditative sip. "You would so. But she and I
don't seem to get around to confidences much. I guess she ought
to marry her brother." It was said without resentment.

"Did she tell you his account of what happened that night?"
Mark nodded.

"Seem to you convincing?"

"Why not? John wouldn't kill anyone. He's too high-minded.
I'd as soon think Charles Reilly had done it. Sooner, in fact."

"What an extraordinary notion! Why Charles, of all people?"

"This was something Sukie *did* confide. Soon after Charles came over, he and Sukie were at some party or other in the House. He invited her to his rooms for a final drink and to show her a rare, privately printed edition of Yeats, ha! *ha!* Then he made a strong pass at her—the old fellow was half-stoned, mind you."

"But what's this to do with Josiah?"

"Patience, dear sir. Charles was getting a darned sight too close, and the rape might have been consummated, when Sukie broke away for a moment and yelled out the window. Who should happen to be passing but brother Josh? He hurried in, banged on the door, and found Sukie in tears and a state of extreme déshabillé."

"It seems an occasion for someone to have slain Charles, rather than vice versa."

"Well, you know, this talk about American violence is exaggerated. And Josh doesn't—didn't work that way. Oh, you mean me? By the time Sukie told me, it had all blown over for her, and Charles had apologized profusely, and they'd made it up. I suspect Sukie rather enjoyed the experience—in retrospect, anyway. Not every graduate student is near-raped by a distinguished Irish poet. She's got very fond of Charles, as you've noticed. Still and all, perhaps she'd have admired me more passionately if I'd called him out even then: they say women do love being fought over."

"But Josiah—"

"I'm coming to that. I'd not drop dead with amazement if you told me he was putting the bite on old Charles."

"Kindly explicate."

"If Josh had told the Master about this, he'd have had to kick Charles out. Now Charles may be a distinguished Irish poet but he's far from being a rich man, and he makes his living by spend-

ing the winter months over here—lucrative readings and lectures.
So, if it got about that he was in the habit of assaulting innocent
young students, his main source of income would dry up on him."

"Are you serious?"

"Well, Josh could be very mean. As I discovered quite young.
He was also a sexual puritan. Add those two qualities up, and
what do you get?—the possibility he might have been holding
Charles's outbreak over his head. Not necessarily for money. For
some subtle satisfaction, maybe. All I'm saying is, Charles had as
good a motive as John Tate—and a more likely disposition—for
stopping Josh's mouth."

"I think I need another drink after that," said Nigel at last.

"Your servant, sir."

"How would you account for Charles's waiting so long before
he decided to silence your brother? A month or more?"

"The Irish have long memories. And he's a devious sort of
fellow, wouldn't you say? Maybe Josh had given him some sort
of final ultimatum—excuse the pleonasm. I just don't know."

"But it wasn't he who had made the appointment."

"How do you know he hadn't made an appointment? Anyway,
what was to stop him from walking right in? The door was
open." For the first time this evening, Mark looked appalled. His
sallow cheeks darkened.

"But you said it was locked when you tried it at 10:15."

"Look here, I'm not *accusing* Charles. I was stating a hypo-
thetical case."

"I'm not."

"Okay. Then Charles locked it after he'd killed Josiah."

"But John Tate arrived after you, and he found it open. Do
you mean there was yet another person in this drove of visitors
who somehow unlocked it between 10:15 and 10:30, leaving it
open for John?"

There was a long pause. "Oh, deary me, and I thought we

were having such an amiable conversation," said Mark finally.

"So you found the door unlocked," Nigel prompted.

Mark remained silent, in a rigid pose.

"All right. I'll tell you," Nigel went on. "You'd received a typewritten note from your brother, asking you to call in at 10:15. You did so. You found the door was *not* locked. You walked in. And—?"

Mark still did not utter a word.

"And we get alternative possibilities. Either you had already visited him earlier, and shot him while the Food Man was bawling. The note never existed. You forgot to lock the door behind you when you left. So why did you return to his staircase a quarter of an hour later, as you were seen to do? Perhaps you remembered you'd left some incriminating clue in the room. Perhaps you were already possessed by the murderer's compulsion to revisit the scene of his crime. The second alternative—"

"No, *I'll* tell you what happened. I did receive the note. I did walk into the office. I found Josh dead." Mark spoke slowly and bleakly. "Why didn't I give the alarm? You'd think it was such a simple, obvious thing to do, wouldn't you? The fact is, I disliked Josh thoroughly. I hated him. D'you know my first reaction when I saw him there dead? Relief. Pleasure. And then, because I'd hated him so much, I felt as if everyone else must know it, and would assume it was me who killed him. He was dead, anyway: I couldn't do anything for him, and—"

"—and, in short, you were afraid?"

"I expect so. Yes, I expect so."

"You deceive yourself then. Hate sounds more respectable than indifference." Mark took his head out of his hands, looking startled. Nigel went on: "You are a cold man. Sukie realizes this instinctively. It's probably your father's treatment of you, but you want to go your own way, to sidestep trouble, not to be involved. I suggest your basic reaction when you saw your brother dead was one of self-defensive indifference—let somebody else take care of this."

"That's a harsh verdict," said Mark musingly: he had the good scholar's power to examine evidence dispassionately. "But analysis of my character is not so urgent right now. The point seems to be, what are you going to do about—?"

There was a loud knocking at the door. "Oh, hell, why can't they leave me alone?" said Mark, rising to open it.

Charles Reilly entered, on a waft of liquor. "What's this I hear about Sukie's brother?" he asked belligerently.

"Well, what *do* you hear?"

"He's been arrested. Would you believe it? Will they hang him, will they?"

"Don't get so excited, Charles," said Mark.

Nigel briefly explained the situation, while Charles took pulls at a half-tumbler of neat whisky he'd poured himself, unasked.

"Well, don't that beat all?" said Charles, running his hand through his thick red hair. "The poor gerrul, to have her brother disgraced!"

"All that's proved yet against him is withholding evidence."

"Ah, now, Nigel me lad, there's no smoke without fire."

"Have you ever sat in a station waiting room, with an alleged fire smoking in the grate? Anyway, we've got smoke rising from too many different places."

"Is that so?" said Charles comfortably. "Well, it must make things more exciting for our resident criminologist."

"But not for our resident poet?"

"I'm sitting out this dance."

"You're remarkably unconcerned, Charles, for someone who had a motive for killing Josiah Ahlberg."

The poet's blue eyes turned from fire to ice. He took another gulp of whisky, and set down his glass very slowly on the table.

"Motive? What can you be blathering about? Sure I hardly knew the fella."

"As St. Peter more or less remarked on another occasion."

"No blasphemy now!"

"I heard today you'd once made a violent pass at Sukie."

"Who the devil told you that?" exclaimed Charles Reilly, turning a suspicious eye upon Mark, who visibly relaxed when Nigel answered, "I heard it through Sukie herself."

Charles was not in a state of mind capable of noticing the curious preposition. "You can never trust a woman not to blab. Or exaggerate. I did lose my head a little one night. But it was nothing—"

"An attempt at rape, and you call it nothing?" cut in Nigel.

Charles's ruddy face darkened. "Now don't you browbeat me. I'm not in the dock. I was about to say, 'it was nothing'—"

"You mean, she rather enjoyed the experience?" said Mark.

Charles shrugged this aside with his bulky shoulders. "Nothing to do with the case of Josiah Ahlberg. Sukie and I—we're on the friendliest terms now, and you know it. All's forgiven and forgotten."

"Forgotten? Including the fact that Josiah caught you with your pants down, so to speak?" asked Nigel.

Charles Reilly glared at him; then, with one of his quick, brilliant smiles, said, "So *that's* my motive? May God forgive you! Wait now, will I tell you what's in your mind? Josiah used this knowledge to blackmail me, so I stopped his mouth for him."

"Did he?"

"He did not. He was heartless as a dead skate, God rest his soul; but no blackmailer."

"That's true, I'm sure," said Mark.

"Not for money, perhaps. What else might there be? . . . Did he approve your engagement to Sukie?" Nigel asked.

"I can't say he did. First there was the row over her brother. And then he didn't like her father's having been a Red. He told me there was bad blood in the family. I daresay he'd warned Chester off Sukie before."

"And your own father would have blown up if Josiah had revealed the scandal? Particularly if he'd put Sukie into a bad light—said she'd welcomed Charles's advances?"

"He certainly would have."

Charles Reilly pushed out his thick lips. "This is all terrible nonsense. Are you saying that Josiah— If he wasn't blackmailing me for money, what in the name of the saints was he trying to get out of me?"

"That's easy. He wanted you to tell his father a story, which he himself would confirm—that Sukie had attempted to seduce *you*. This would compel Mark to break off the engagement. If you refused, Josiah would tell the real facts to the authorities: you'd lose your job—and the chance of any more such jobs in the States. Moral turpitude is something the immigration people don't care for."

Charles had been studying Nigel with mounting astonishment and admiration. "Now that's the most ingenious tale I ever heard. You should be writing books. Though I will say, if Josiah had tried anything like that, I'd have been sorely tempted to shoot him. We had a short way with informers in the Trouble."

"You were in the I.R.A., Charles?"

"I was. Where else would I have been?"

"Well, I'm an informer myself. I'll be passing on your stories to Lieutenant Brady. You both know that."

Mark volunteered the comment that Lieutenant Brady could stuff it. Charles began to protest, but then fell silent. Turning at the door Nigel said, "I hope, for your sakes, both your stories are true. Brady'll be interviewing you tomorrow, I expect, and he's a very intelligent man."

"And you said *I* am cold" was Mark's parting shot.

But they are intelligent men too, Nigel reflected as he crossed the court: so it's strange how relatively painless it was to extract this new information from them. It's more understandable with Mark; he's an academic, with a built-in escape route from the real world; but Charles had once been a man of action. Neither of them seems to realize the danger he is in. Perhaps it's because they're both innocent and cannot take the idea of their being under suspicion at all seriously. Perhaps one of them was playing a deep game with me, concealing his actual moves beneath a flow of easy patter.

Nigel opened his door, turned on the light, and went to the telephone.

8 ☞ The Superimposed Redhead

Arriving in Hall next morning for breakfast, Nigel saw the Master and the Senior Tutor at a distant table. Most of the students had already breakfasted and left for their first lectures or seminars of the day. Zeke beckoned to Nigel to join him: Nigel carried his tray, piled high with two miniature cartons of cornflakes, milk, two glasses of fruit juice, two fried eggs (sunny side up), and several slices of bread, and sat down.

"I don't know how you can do it," said the Master, staring at this assortment. "You know Donald?"

The Senior Tutor, a lanky, sardonic man, looking almost as young as some of the students, rose and shook hands.

"We've been talking about the Ahlbergs. Messy business. Josiah murdered and someone playing practical jokes on Chester," said Zeke.

The Senior Tutor's mouth twitched. "It certainly was a humdinger."

"No ideas about the culprit on that?" asked Nigel.

"None. All we know is that one of the serving women noticed the placard on the door when she came in to ready things for breakfast. I've traced the issue of *Playboy* in which the luscious redhead exhibits herself and someone has looked through all the students' rooms, but found no copy of the magazine with that photograph cut out: anyway, he'd have taken care to get rid of it."

"What about the Faculty?" asked Nigel, eating vigorously.

"You mean as the joker? Oh, I think not, though a misguided alumnus presented us with a year's subscription to the magazine, for the Senior Common Room. I didn't care for the implication that we're a sex-starved bunch of elderly *voyeurs*."

"So you're assuming the joker is a student."

"Nigel!" protested the Master. "You can't suppose for a moment it's one of us?"

"I don't see why not, if it was done out of malice rather than high spirits. Chester has suffered before from this sort of thing. You'd know, Donald, if anyone had it in for him—tutor or student?"

"In for Chester? The answer is negative. I made some inquiries—tactful, hopefully—among the students. It's a mystery to them. Chester hasn't flunked anyone lately. They think of him as a nice-enough guy, not very conversable, unobtrusive almost to the vanishing point. What's most in his favor, from their angle, is that he takes them as seriously as they take themselves."

"So you're at a dead end?"

"We're not a preparatory school," said the Master. "We can't apply sanctions—detention for every boy till the culprit confesses. You said just now '*tutor* or student.' You would agree, would you, Donald, that Chester has no ill-wishers among the Faculty?"

"He certainly hasn't, as far as *I* can judge. He's too unnoticeable to make enemies."

"Yet *someone* seems to be laying for him," Nigel broke into his second egg. "What d'you call them when they're lying flat on their faces? 'Sunny side down'?"

The two eminent scholars were at a loss for a reply.

Nigel said, "I happened to see a copy of *Playboy* here, with an illustration cut out, and—"

"And it was that cunning redhead?" asked Donald.

"It was. I verified it later, from a copy on a newsstand."

"But, Nigel, why didn't you tell us? Whose room was it in?"

"Not a student's. Sorry, Zeke, but I've got to play this my own way. These practical jokes may be linked up with the murder of Josiah." Nigel suddenly stared into vacancy. "Oh, my God, the pistol!" he cried.

Master and Senior Tutor convulsively turned their heads, half expecting to see a masked gunman behind them.

"Must you?" exclaimed Donald. "You've given me a heart condition."

"The mailboxes! Why didn't it occur to me before?"

"Take it easy!" said Donald in a humoring tone. "What about the mailboxes?"

Nigel explained. "You know they're six inches deep and a little over a foot long. The shape of a shoebox. Don't you see?—you could get a pistol or a small revolver into one of them."

"Sure you could," said Donald. "And the next time the mailman opened it to put letters in, he'd find a gun there. Surprise, surprise!"

"You could put it in a long envelope."

"And what about the actual owner of the mailbox?" asked Zeke. "Wouldn't he find it there?"

"Aren't there any unused ones in the House?" Nigel asked.

The Senior Tutor thought it over. "Let's see. The guest rooms haven't been occupied this fortnight. And there's Rubin's: hasn't come back yet: illness."

"Hm. Well, Donald, will you have those boxes opened now? If you find a gun, don't touch it. Shut the box and tell me."

The Senior Tutor loped off, looking skeptical.

"But, Nigel, you can't open a mailbox unless you know the combination," said Zeke.

"Oh, they're not such a deadly secret. After all, someone knew the combination of Chester's, to put that offensive object into it. Damn, I never thought of the obvious one."

"Whose?"

"Josiah's. I bet no one's opened *it* since his death."

"Then you lose your stake. Brady told the Superintendent to open it every day and hand over the mail to him."

"Oh," said Nigel, somewhat dashed. He was still more so when the Senior Tutor returned five minutes later, wearing an expression of skepticism justified.

"You're right off target this time. They're all empty."

"Box, *et praeterea nihil*," commented the Master. "Sorry you've been troubled, Senior Tutor."

"You're welcome, sir." . . .

It was to turn out a disturbed day for Nigel. Hardly was he back in his room when Lieutenant Brady telephoned, with the news that he was coming to interview Mark and Charles in the afternoon, and that Mr. Ahlberg senior desired Mr. Strangeways to come and see him.

"What the devil does *he* want of me?"

"He desires to be informed about the progress of the case."

"But *I'm* not handling the case. Why doesn't he ask you?"

"He does. Three times a day at least," Brady muttered.

"Now, look here, Brady—"

"I just thought, seeing as you extracted some useful evidence from Mark, you might find the old—Mr. Ahlberg senior's angle on the crime valuable."

"So you've wished him on to me. I don't believe he ever asked to see me."

"You'll ring him and make an appointment, then? He's stopping at the Brabourne Hotel."

"He can ring me," snorted Nigel, "and make his own bloody appointment—to see me here."

There was a discreet cough over the telephone. "He's a man who expects people to come to him, not vice versa. And he's a fairly impatient type."

"Well, he can damn well wait." Nigel banged down the receiver.

The next moment, a memory broke surface. "We can wait." The legend on the wall of the funeral parlor. Chester swerving his car dangerously when Nigel read it out loud that afternoon on the way to Amherst.

"We can wait." Had that cautious, if unlucky, driver shied to hear his own secret thought repeated by Nigel? "Can wait," till father dies. His dough, plus Josiah's share (if Josiah predeceased him) coming to us. Worth waiting for. The "we" would be Mark and himself. Supposing the pair were in collusion to kill Josiah?

What would follow from this hypothesis? Nigel ruminated. Chester flies off to England, leaving Mark to do the deed; thus any suspicion they had planned it together would be diminished. Afterward each of them had behaved quite naturally, each dismissing the idea that his brother could be a murderer. Of the two, Mark had seemed more distressed by Josiah's death—as of course he would if his distress and revulsion were the aftermath of a murder committed by his own hand.

But these two men, though very different in personality, share a common trait of the academic mind: they tend toward a certain unworldliness or lack of "realism"; they have to convert human problems into abstractions before they can deal with them. Now, supposing two such characters wished to block any idea that there could be criminal collusion between them, might they not decide to do so—theoretical as ever, but more subtle than the common run of criminals—not by quarreling violently in public, but by drawing a more sophisticated red herring across the trail?

Who could suspect a couple of conspiracy to murder, one of

whom was making the other a victim of secret persecution, playing juvenile practical jokes on him?

Mark would certainly know the combination of Chester's mailbox. It was Mark who had possessed the mutilated copy of *Playboy,* and left it lying on his table for me to discover. The nature of these jokes points to Mark, with his streak of immaturity and puckishness, as the one who thought them up. Maybe he had planted the horde of cockroaches in Chester's room, too. When Chester had said, "I don't have persecution mania, I'm persecuted," he was deliberately sowing a seed in my mind.

On this theory, the practical jokes are a last line of defense: Mark would only fall back on it if he felt himself hard pressed by the police investigation. This had happened as a result of the student's seeing him near Josiah's room on the night of the murder. But why had he returned there at 10:15, only eight minutes after shooting his brother? Shelve that one for the present. If Mark is in danger, he allows me to discover him as the author of the jokes, trusting me as a friend to hush it up. So I must play along with him.

It was Mark's friendliness (which had survived even the conversation of last night) that stuck in Nigel's throat. He genuinely liked Mark—that was the trouble—and it was little use reminding himself that murderers sometimes are likable men. Nigel had nothing against Chester either, for the matter of that; except that he seemed a stuffed man, a bit of a bore, a bit unreal—and vaguely pathetic in his unreality.

The telephone bell wrenched Nigel away from his thoughts. It was Sukie, sounding breathless and rather tearful.

"They've been at me again. I must see you, Nigel. Can I come and see you now?"

Ten minutes later he heard feet running up the stairs. He opened the door. Sukie ran into his arms, and buried her head on his shoulder, sobbing.

"I'm so miserable! I hate it all. I can't go on any longer."

Nigel put her in an armchair and sat on the arm of it, holding her hand, till she began to recover.

"You've had Brady round?" he asked.

"Not him. Two men from his homicide squad. They asked me questions for an hour, trying to trap me into admitting I'd hidden John. They even said he'd confessed that I knew where he was hiding."

"But you didn't believe them?"

"I certainly did *not*. John would never betray me," she said proudly, tears still shining in her eyes.

"So that's all right."

"But it isn't," cried Sukie. "They'll accuse him of the murder. I know they will. Oh, *why* did he ever go to see Josiah? To think I arranged it for him!"

"They won't—not without a good deal more evidence."

"They will though. That god-awful old brute is yelling them on—you know, Mark's father. Mark told me so himself yesterday."

"What's he got against John?"

"It's all of us he hates. Me as much as anyone. He's a John Birch type, a total reactionary. He'd think it a fate worse than death for Mark to—to be married to me."

"But surely that wouldn't influence Mark?"

"Oh, I guess not. I hope not. But he's so *weak* in some ways." Sukie put down Nigel's hand, decisively as if it was a book and she had finished a chapter. She went to stand by the mantelshelf, her eyes glittering at him feverishly. "You *must* find the real murderer."

Nigel gazed back at her in silence. At last he said, "Suppose the real murderer turned out to be Mark?"

The lovely gray eyes seemed to glaze over for a moment. *"Mark!"* she said then. "But that's absurd."

"He's one of the suspects. And he knows it. Has he never talked to you about it?"

"No. No, he hasn't. I don't think he'd want to—to— And he is very, very reticent about things. I wish I knew him better," she added quickly.

"If you had to choose between him and John?"

Sukie looked at him for a moment—then smiled uneasily. "What a thing to ask. That's like one of those cute questions in the Practical Ethics course—'If your wife and your only child were drowning, which would you rescue?' "

"All right. Well, forget it," said Nigel briskly. "Now tell me about you and Charles Reilly."

Her eyes dilated; then she drooped her long lashes and began to blush. "Who—who told you about *that?*"

"Mark. And Charles."

"Well, honestly!—"

"Are you in an honest frame of mind today, Sukie?" asked Nigel, very seriously.

"You know I am."

"Then tell me the truth about this: after Josiah found you in Charles's clutches, did he at any time refer to it again?"

"No. I don't believe I ever met him again, even."

"I knew Charles apologized, and you made it up with him. Has he ever suggested to you since that Josiah might be going to make trouble for him—or for you—over the episode?"

"Of course not. Never. What makes you ask? Oh, my gracious, do the police suspect Charles *too?*" But she said it with no noticeable concern and wandered around the room, then stopped and pointed to a cardboard basset hound on the mantelshelf, with a plastic tear fastened to its eye and the legend I MISS YOU inscribed beneath. "My, will you look at this cunning dog! How darling. And someone misses you. Does he belong to you at home?"

"Yes. Clare sent it me. In a satirical moment."

"Oh. Doesn't she love you then?"

"Indeed she does."

The girl considered him. "I can see why she would. I guess I do too. I seem to go for father figures."

"Well, that's fine, Sukie dear. But beware of ill-digested psychological terms."

"Aren't you a pedantic old man," she said, smiling sweetly.

"I am not," replied Nigel, faintly nettled.

She walked straight up to him, fitted her body against his, and gave him a long, long kiss. She was breathing fast.

"Do you usually kiss your father figures like this?" asked Nigel, when he had gently pushed her away to arm's length.

"Wouldn't you like to know? Well, I must be on my way. 'Bye." Sukie turned at the door, smiled at him—brilliantly, a little complacently—and was gone.

More complications, grumbled Nigel to himself. Unpredictable girl. What's she cooking up now? Have to read women between the lines—the printed text is seldom reliable. I wouldn't put it past her to have set fire to old Charles quite deliberately. As an experiment. The young like playing with fire. Curiosity—all right so long as they don't elevate it into highfaluting, doctrinaire nonsense about the Right to Experience. I wonder how much Sukie's had.

The telephone rang again. It was the Master to say that Mr. Ahlberg senior would be lunching with him, and hoped it would be convenient if he called upon Mr. Strangeways at 2:15.

"Do you quote or is that a tactful paraphrase? All right, we'll give him an audience."

"And, Nigel, if you don't have any kid gloves, go out and buy a pair. Remember, he's the-founder-of-this-House."

Sharp at 2:15, the great man arrived with the Master, who made the introductions in his most poker-faced manner and withdrew. Nigel muttered some conventional condolence, but Mr.

Ahlberg cut it short with a brusque movement of his hand.

"Now, tell me, what is your opinion, as an outsider, of the discipline in this House?" asked Mr. Ahlberg in a flat midwestern accent, poking his head at Nigel like a tortoise.

"The tone seems excellent. As an outsider, I'm really not competent to speak about the discipline. And the Master is an old friend of mine."

"You academics always stick together," Ahlberg said testily. "Like a swarm of bees. Brady tells me you've had some experience in these matters."

"These— Oh, you mean detective work? Yes, that is so."

"I don't have much confidence in him. If I were satisfied with *your* credentials, I'd be prepared to hire you, at double your usual fees, to prove the case against my son's murderer."

"But, Mr. Ahlberg, I'm not for sale," said Nigel mildly.

"Oh, rot! That's for the birds."

"Every man has his price?" Nigel asked softly.

"Show me one man who hasn't."

Nigel surveyed his would-be employer. Mr. Ahlberg had Chester's small body: the features of his wrinkled, tortoise face carried a distant echo of Josiah's. He wore a black suit, a black tie, an old-fashioned high starched collar.

"I gather what you're asking me to do is to prove a case against John Tate."

"Who else?" answered the old man with appalling frankness. "That young man is trash, just like the rest of his family. I had inquiries made when Chester'd got himself involved with the sister. Trash, I tell you. And the young ruffian had the impudence to accuse Josiah of—" The bloodless old lips munched into incoherence.

"But, Mr. Ahlberg, nothing can be *proved* against John Tate until the police find the gun or else break him down. I could do nothing about that. And *I'm* not convinced he is guilty."

"Huh? Ah, those Tates are paying you, are they?"

"You seem to have money on the brain. You accuse me first of being an academic, secondly of being venal. Neither charge is true." Nigel's contemptuous tone penetrated the tortoise carapace. Mr. Ahlberg glanced at him with something like respect.

"I see, I see. Well, then forget it. I like a fellow who stands up to me. I guess I've too many yes men in my employ. However, my offer holds good."

"To find the murderer, or to prove murder against John Tate?"

"What's the difference?" Ahlberg asked.

"Tate is not the only suspect."

"Fiddle!"

"There's quite a strong case against Mark, for instance."

"*My son?* This is outrageous! Brady never told me—"

"I don't imagine he'd have the nerve."

"Then you'd better tell me."

Nigel gave a carefully edited version of his theories about Mark. The old man questioned him keenly at certain points; but his initial incredulity turned to uneasiness, and he said at last, "I've not been too happy about Mark. I'll admit it. I tried to bring him up, and Chester too, with a respect for discipline, for duty. But he was always going his own way—saying yes, but meaning no. People said I was too severe with them both; but it was only for their own good. I feared at one time Mark was becoming a playboy, but fortunately he seemed to have settled down here. Josiah was keeping an eye on him—and Chester of course—in loco parentis."

"You know Josiah's half brothers resented that. They disliked his talebearing to you, his taking your side against them always."

"Maybe, maybe," said the old man grimly, "but you don't kill your brother for talebearing."

"Did Josiah ever say anything to you about Mark's relationship with Miss Tate? Or Chester's?"

"I believe he'd persuaded Chester to sever the relationship last spring. And he wrote me a month or two ago, saying he believed he could deal with Mark if necessary."

"Considering that Mark and Chester favored the same girl—have they always been very close?"

"I should say never. They're very, very different types, of course. Chester was never wild: he gave no trouble; and unfortunately he cut no ice either. I shouldn't say it about my own son, but he's a cipher and I'm afraid he always will be. A zero. I wanted to put him into one of my concerns when he left college, but instead he has to become a *teacher*." Mr. Ahlberg spat out the opprobrious word with the utmost contempt.

"Very distressing for you."

"Don't misunderstand me. I approve of education. I built this House for Cabot, didn't I? Josiah was highly esteemed in the world of scholarship. But teaching in a Business School! You might as well spend your life playing at toy soldiers." The tortoise had shot forward on the scrawny neck. "I'm an old man, Mr. Strangeways. If Mark got into bad trouble, it would kill me. You must see to it that he doesn't."

"You've a soft spot for him, in spite of everything?"

"I guess you're right. Mark's got some of his old dad's red blood in him. But he knows on which side his bread is buttered. There've been some violent episodes in his past, and perhaps he could have killed a man in hot blood, but he'd never do it in a treacherous way—not like poor Josiah was killed." The old man's flat voice shook.

"I hope you're right, Mr. Ahlberg."

Josiah's father departed shortly after, leaving Nigel to contemplate this strange mixture of the shrewd, the maudlin, the autocratic and the wildly erroneous to which he had been treated. He sat for a long time, trying to separate out Mr. Ahlberg's qualities and trace each one to Josiah, Mark or Chester. It was a sterile occupation. . . .

Late that afternoon Mark called to him from the court beneath his window and Nigel invited him up.

"How did it go?" Nigel asked.

"Brady let me off. Provisionally. With a caution. Don't withhold evidence again, or— The fact is, he's baffled. The fact is, I'm much more frightened of you—the way you turn this whole affair into an intellectual game and trap your friends, the suspects, into playing with you."

"Do you mean to say that Brady's willing to pass over your finding Josiah's body and saying nothing about it?"

"Seemingly. I dare say he's just paying out more rope for me to hang myself with. Still, I'll say it's a relief right now. And I have the benefit of a quiet conscience. Unless some son of a bitch frames some real *evidence* against me, why should I worry?" Mark Ahlberg, the interview behind him, was in a manic phase, beaming, sparkling, carefree.

"You didn't see your father? He was lunching with Zeke. I had a chat with him."

"Did you now? What was he trying to sell you?"

"He was trying to buy me—he wants John Tate sent to the chair, and you saved from it."

"Very loyal. What else?" Mark asked.

"He told me he approves of education. And he clearly has a certain unwilling admiration for you."

"Really? Since when?"

"He thinks of you as a chip—a very small chip—off the old block. A playboy who has sobered up. I thought it would be unkind to reveal to him your low passion for cheesecake."

"My what?"

"You subscribe to *Playboy,* don't you?"

"I don't subscribe to it; I have bought a copy occasionally. Why?"

"There was one on your table the other day. It seems to have disappeared, by the way."

Mark looked politely uninterested.

"The trouble is, it had a picture cut out of it. And the same picture—that stunning nude redhead—was stuck onto the photograph of Chester. The one some joker pinned on the Hall door."

Mark gazed at Nigel incredulously. His mouth opened and closed. He shook his head, as though a fly were tormenting him. "Are you suggesting that *I* faked up that poster?" he said at last.

"My dear Mark, it's no concern of mine if you tease your brother."

"But I didn't!" Mark burst out. "I didn't! *I* wouldn't do a ridiculous thing like that. It's not adult. The Faculty just don't go around making monkeys of one another in such a childish way. The idea is *utterly* crazy. Why, I'd be out on my neck in a minute, if— Do you think anyone would risk his job for the sake of playing such a juvenile trick?"

"No. Not for that."

An apprehensive look came into Mark's face. "My God! What I was saying—it looks as though someone *is* trying to frame evidence against me."

9 ☞ "A Funeral in My Brain"

Lieutenant Brady was a worried man. He paced Nigel's room as if it were a prison cell. "These people get me down. I can deal with hoods. I know how their minds work. But college instructors!—they're always at least one jump ahead. They have all the answers, or think they do. Like talking books they are."

"You let Mark Ahlberg off the hook, he tells me."

"I could pull him in, but what's the use? So he goes into his brother's room and finds him dead. So he walks out again, washes his hands of it. It could be. If he'd shot him already, what did he come back for?"

"Anxiety? Afraid he'd left some clue behind?"

Brady shook his head dispiritedly. "I've worked on him. I had men working on him since the killing. There is nothing, repeat nothing, to connect him with it."

"Except motive and opportunity. So you're letting him loose in the hope he'll do something silly? Like killing his other brother?"

Brady shot Nigel a sharp green glance. "It could happen. I just wish he'd rid me of Pa Ahlberg first. The old s.o.b. clings to me like a hairshirt."

"Have you thought the two brothers might be in collusion?"

"Now, isn't that a sweet idea! Tell me all about it."

Nigel spoke for some time. Tried out on Brady, the theory did not sound so brilliant. When he reached the practical-joke aspect of it, the Lieutenant gave his harsh bark of laughter.

"So it's got you too—this academic fantasy building. How did Mark react when you told him he'd been wishing redheads onto his brother?"

"He denied it. He appeared deeply shocked."

"Uh-huh."

"But the fact remains: he had this copy of *Playboy,* and he doesn't have it any longer. He thinks somebody must be planting evidence on him."

"I'd believe anything in a madhouse like this," Brady said. "Anything except a guy persecuting his brother to prove the two of them didn't knock off a third. Have you any more crazy suggestions for me? What about Master Edwardes? Maybe he had some scandal he didn't want exposed. Maybe Josiah caught him in bed with the President's wife."

"I *can* supply a sex angle. But it's probably only a subplot. You interview Charles Reilly?"

"The red-haired guy? Writes poetry? Sure—routine questions. Why?"

"Josiah caught him trying to rape Sukie Tate."

Brady stared. "Well, what do you know! You should be writing for the tabloids, Mr. Strangeways."

Nigel told him the story. "There could be a motive there. And Reilly was in the I.R.A. Those chaps were quick on the trigger."

The telephone rang. It was a call for Brady. When he had taken the message, he turned to Nigel. "There's another of your beautiful theories liquidated. No one answering to Chester Ahlberg's name or description flew in from Britain that night. Two of my men have been toting photographs of him around the airport: they tried passenger lists, customs control and the passport desk; they even rustled up some stewardesses on the possible international flights. Nothing. They're good men, they don't make mistakes."

"Well, that seems to eliminate Chester. Have you got any further with John Tate?"

"He's a queer cookie. The psycho says he has manic-depressive tendencies. The doc's been working on him hard, trying to get a coherent story of where he was between finding the body and giving himself up. We've quite an itinerary now—young Tate's memory seems to be improving. We haven't found any witness yet who's certain he saw him. We're still going 'round cafés and eateries which Tate thinks he may have visited."

"In case he got rid of a gun there?"

"I have to investigate his story. Helps to fend off Pa Ahlberg. Not that I believe it—not one little bit."

Nigel felt sorry about having sent a sizable section of the homicide squad on a wild-goose chase, but it was too late now to disillusion them. His bad conscience made him a little aggressive. "Sukie Tate tells me your men tried to break her down by saying John had confessed. I don't like that."

Brady's gaze was hard. "We're investigating a murder, not playing checkers. What's this girl to you anyway?"

"A girl."

"She was hiding him? She knew where he was hidden?"

"If that is true, it's irrelevant. You've got him now. Look, Brady, do you honestly think he's a murderer?"

"No comment."

Nigel sighed. "It'd do no harm to turn the heat on Charles Reilly for a change."

"You think *he's* a murderer?"

"No comment." . . .

"Charles was stopping last night with friends in Concord. I

thought I'd drive out and bring him back this evening. Would you care to accompany me?"

"That'd be very nice, Chester. Thank you."

"I'm sorry Mark can't make it. He'd be a more knowledgeable guide for a literary pilgrimage."

Nigel politely declined any excessive enthusiasm for literary pilgrimages, and confessed to having never read *Walden*.

Chester seemed disappointed. "But the woods should be very colorful at this time of year," he said.

They drove out of the city in brilliant sunshine, a vapor trail fraying out in the blue sky far overhead. Chester, in a suit of funereal black and black kid gloves, a fedora on his head, negotiated the Sunday forenoon traffic with his usual care. The car heater was turned to full strength: Nigel, feeling drowsy already, settled down to a boring ride, and possible lecture.

"I had a talk with your father," he said finally, to keep himself awake.

Chester did not withdraw his eyes from the road ahead. "Is that so? You know I feel that he stood up to the ordeal remarkably well for a man of his age."

"So did I," said Nigel.

"I didn't realize you had attended the funeral."

"Oh, I see what you mean. No, I didn't, I'm afraid. It must have been a notable—er—occasion," Nigel hurriedly added.

Chester enumerated the academic dignitaries who had been present, and gave a synopsis of the President's valedictory address.

Presently they were driving through a New England village, passing a white clapboard church with an elegant spire, and a graveyard beside it.

"What I don't seem able to get out of my head is the noise the clods make dropping on the coffin," said Chester unexpectedly. "It's so final—and yet so sort of banal. At the time, I couldn't work up any response. It was like—like being anesthetized."

Nigel quoted:

> "I felt a funeral in my brain
> And mourners to and fro,
> Kept treading, treading, till it seemed
> That sense was breaking through.
> And when they all were seated,
> A service like a drum
> Kept beating, beating, till I thought
> My mind was going numb."

"Yes," said Chester soberly. "That's very apposite."

"The mourners shuttling back and forth. An image of the ineluctable and the futile. What's the matter, Chester? Are you feeling all right?"

Chester braked to the roadside and opened a window.

"Sorry. I guess I was momentarily overcome."

"The car *is* very hot."

"Josiah and I had our differences. But blood is thicker than water. And when—when your brother dies, he takes a piece of your past away with him—a piece of your foundations."

Autumn wind blew through the car, frozen and pine-scented. Shivering, Chester closed the window, drove on. They stopped later at a wayside café, where Nigel devoured blueberry doughnuts and a jumbo-size chocolate ice cream, and his companion ate a carefully chosen, well-balanced lunch which, Nigel felt, must have scrupulously followed some dietitian's chart. At Concord, Chester made straight for the woods, which on this fall Sunday wore a Joseph's coat of color, maple, sumac and birch leaves predominating. They walked down the track to the edge of the lake, which curved away into the distance, and sat down to admire a scene unchanged since Thoreau had gazed at it from his hermit's hut. The tension seemed to have drained away out of

Chester's face: he breathed in the pure air deeply: his body relaxed: he had the expression of one who is playing truant from routine preoccupations.

The beauties of nature, however, though they could attract Nigel, seldom held him long. He turned to the proper study of mankind. "Mark taking Sukie out for the day?"

Chester made an effort to return to the everyday world. "I believe he planned to."

"I suppose there'll not be the same opposition to their marrying now."

"There won't? I don't see—why, father *surely* hasn't changed his views about that, has he? Did he say something to that effect to you?"

"I was thinking of Josiah. He was very hostile too, Sukie told me."

Chester looked puzzled. Frowned. "*That*'s rather an overstatement."

"Well, he seems to have put obstacles in the way, when *you* had an understanding with her."

"Oh, there was nothing definite as far as I was concerned, you know," said Chester evasively. "In any event, Mark suits her better."

"I wouldn't have thought *he* was serious enough. She's such an earnest girl. Rather overpowering. She can't approve of Mark's frivolous side, can she?"

Chester stirred uncomfortably. "I've not discussed him with her. And Mark generally gets what he wants."

"The Joker takes the Queen?"

A birch leaf eddied down onto Chester's knee. He did not brush it off.

"I don't quite get you."

"Well, he was a great joker in his young days, wasn't he?" Nigel paused to light a cigarette. "The question is—is he still?"

"Mark is a fully responsible member of society," replied Chester firmly.

"So it's just a coincidence that he had a copy of *Playboy* with that nude cut out—the one used with your photograph on the poster?"

Chester went rigid, staring at him: the left corner of his mouth trembled, and he put up a hand to cover it. "But that's—I just cannot believe it. Are you sure of your facts?"

"Quite sure."

"But what does *he* say? There must be some explanation."

"He says someone must have planted it on him."

"Well, naturally. What else could it have been?"

"That copy of *Playboy* has since disappeared. If someone else planted it on Mark, why should that person bother to remove it?"

A fitful breeze ruffled the pewter surface of Walden Pond. It was like the Americans, thought Nigel irrelevantly, to call a considerable lake a pond.

"No, no. Really, I would never believe it of Mark." Chester's eyes had a haunted look, though, and he spoke like one trying too hard to convince himself.

"There have been other practical jokes played on you this year. Was it a habit of Mark's when he was younger?"

"Well, I suppose you might say— I guess so. He liked to tease me. But it was just high spirits—I never held it against him, you know; that was just Mark. He hazed Josiah too, once or twice."

"But this is a different matter," Nigel persisted. "Whoever's been doing it, it's not out of high spirits: emotional immaturity, perhaps, but that would only shape the pattern—it would not provide the motive. Is there any history of insanity in your family?"

Chester looked startled and somewhat affronted. "There certainly is *not*," he protested.

"Are you sure?" Nigel asked quietly.

"Mark has always been *perfectly* sane."

"What about yourself?"

Chester flushed. "You do ask the *most* extraordinary questions. I don't see why you feel— Well, if you must know, I had a nervous breakdown when I was seventeen. But I don't see what—"

"Paranoia?"

"Now see here, Nigel, I resent this—this—it's indecent."

"But it's very much to the point. Did anyone outside your family know about this breakdown?"

"I guess not. And the doctors, of course."

"So, if someone wanted to disturb your mind again, he would— Oh, perhaps he'd encourage you to feel you were being persecuted. Practical jokes are a fairly sinister form of persecution."

Chester's hands, still in the black kid gloves, dangled between his knees as he sat, bowed forward.

"And no one outside your family knows of the previous breakdown," pressed Nigel.

"Okay, okay, you don't have to spell it out. But there must be something wrong. Why should Mark do this to *me?* There's no *sense* in it. It's just inconceivable."

"Oh, no, it isn't. My dear Chester, I'll be quite crude about it. If you were out of the way, out of your mind, in a bin, and your half brother dead, who would get your father's fortune?"

A rictus, like a dreadful smile, controlled Chester's mouth. Two squirrels ran madly up a tree near the lakeside to their left. Two lovers, enlaced, sauntered past, glancing incuriously at Nigel.

"I thought you were joking the other day when you said I must watch out for Mark." Chester's voice was all but inaudible.

"Did I?"

"It's just a theory, isn't it?" said Chester more strongly. "You don't really believe it?"

"Just a theory."

As if reassured by Nigel's last words, Chester jumped to his feet, scuffed childishly for a few minutes in a drift of fallen leaves, and finally suggested they should go and see the sights of Concord. During the short drive Nigel covertly studied his driver's profile. Chester, seen from this angle, was tolerably good-looking, in a miniature way: thin lips, well-formed nose, small ears. Resemblance to papa? A faint self-satisfaction, maybe, in the set of the mouth? Like his room, Chester's features were tidy to a fault. Was there a certain quirkishness, all too well controlled, beneath his circumspection and conventionality? He was smooth, certainly; yet today again Nigel had been surprised by the cracks that could suddenly appear in this smooth surface. But what was the pressure that cracked the surface? It was difficult to imagine Chester an emotional volcano, holding himself in by Herculean repression.

At Concord, with the aid of a town map which Chester took from his glove compartment, they tracked down the houses where Thoreau, Emerson, Hawthorne and Louisa Alcott had lived. Then, in the Sleepy Hollow cemetery, they found the more permanent residences of those worthies. The graveyard, lying up and down among trees, was dotted with miniature Stars and Stripes marking the resting places of American soldiers. The sightseers, here as in the town, were quiet, orderly, more like researchers in a library than people on a Sunday outing: it was wrong to suppose that Americans lived only in the present and the future; they had, unlike many Europeans, a conscious proprietary respect for their past—perhaps because they were still learning it, recreating it. Nigel thought suddenly of Faulkner in Mississippi, absorbedly tracing the history of one small region, like a lover feeling along the contours of his mistress's face.

Chester, who seemed to have quite recovered from the dumps, was very much the guide and teacher and took Nigel firmly to see the bronze statue of the Minuteman by the river bridge, commemorating the first victory of these American farmers in the War of Independence. " 'The shot heard round the world,' " Chester quoted. "From here, we drove your redcoats back onto Lexington."

Nigel studied the statue. "That's not a bad statue, as statues go. Not bad at all. There's a place for heroics. Though in this case," he added, "it was brother shooting brother."

It was said without *arrière pensée,* but Chester's face went small and tight for a moment. Then he relaxed again. "Can't we forget it, just for an hour?" he asked, smiling ruefully.

Nigel blinked, then said quickly, "I'm sorry, Chester. I was thinking of that war. It was a kind of civil war, after all."

"It was, in a way. It taught us our strength, though. That had to happen."

A small boy holding a large camera asked them politely if they would step aside; he wanted to photograph the Minuteman.

They walked away, past a stand selling hot dogs and peanuts. The leaves were yellow overhead: the river curved an arm behind them, asleep in the late sunshine.

"Taxation without representation," Chester persisted. "That's what we protested. But you Britishers could only treat us as a mob of unruly colonials. The way you did the Irish."

"Well, we learned better. We do learn."

"You've learned how to hand over power gracefully when it has already slipped out of your grasp," said Chester provocatively. "But you haven't always known how to handle it."

"You're impressed by power? As such?"

"Sometimes power is needed. Sometimes the masses want to be governed. Only a few people these days have the flair, or the nerve, for exercising power."

"You'd like to go into politics?"

"Maybe I will, at that."

"I'd have thought you were more cut out to be the strong man behind the scenes—an *éminence grise*—in a country that equates power with money."

"What's wrong with money?" Chester asked sternly.

"Nothing. It's how you get it, or keep it, that can be immoral."

"Money," pronounced Chester, "is the lifeblood of Western civilization—money, and what flows from it—improved communications, medicine, scientific and technological advance, a high standard of living." Chester's eyes glittered: he was fairly launched on what must have been a routine pep talk to his Business School students. Nigel listened, not too attentively, fighting down his natural inclination to regard businessmen as the dregs of the earth. This was a very different and for him a much less interesting Chester than the one who could not forget the noise of the clods falling on his brother's coffin.

"What will you do with your father's fortune," he asked presently, "when it comes your way?"

Chester grinned an almost puckish grin. "Oh, I have several projects in mind."

"Philanthropic?" Nigel grinned too.

"You could say so. In the ultimate issue, they should prove highly beneficial to the nation."

Oh, well, if he wants to be pompous and cagey, let him, thought Nigel; what he means is, after he's skimmed off the cream, there may be some milk to share out among the rest.

"It's at the managerial level," began Chester, "that so many of even your biggest combines are deficient. . . ." He talked Nigel the rest of the way back to the car and into Concord. To the substance of the discourse, Nigel closed the valves of his attention, as Emily Dickinson said, like stone: to its undertones, though, he remained attentive; Chester's enthusiasm for his projects was as great as his confidence in his own powers to implement them. Whether it was the self-confidence of genius or the self-dramatizing fantasy of the child, Nigel could not determine. One thing became clear: Chester would be far wealthier than Nigel had imagined; and his approach, in contrast with his father's technique of grab and shovel, would be that of a highly sophisticated computer. Perhaps Papa Ahlberg had grossly underestimated this son; but equally, it could be that Chester's financial dream palaces were all too insubstantial, begotten by wishful thinking upon complacent abstraction. . . .

"I hope you enjoyed your visit," said Chester, when, after the culture and the high finance, they had picked up Charles Reilly and started the drive home.

"Enjoyed?" Charles gloomily replied. "I was made to read my poems."

"I'd have thought that would suit you down to the ground," said Nigel.

"I have no objection to reading my poems when *I'm* the center of attention," snarled Charles.

"But surely you were?"

"I was not. My host writes verses," said Charles with a baleful intonation. "The fella just used me as an excuse for weighing in with his own paltry scribbles. He read them for hours and hours last night: he'd be reading them still if I hadn't pushed over the table with all the drinks on it. By accident."

"Irish bards and American poetasters," laughed Nigel.

"Mark says Silas Engelbert has quite a reputation," Chester put in.

"Silas Engelbert can neither write poetry nor read it, I tell you." Charles was fierce. "He's nothing more than a vocal masturbator, in love with his own organ. If you can call a scrannel pipe an organ."

They drove steadily on through the darkening countryside. Charles relapsed into gloomy mutterings on the back seat until Chester fished a pint bottle from the glove compartment and handed it to him. "Will this cheer you up, Charles?"

"A *miá's* took me," growled the poet between gulps.

"A mee-aw? What's that?" Nigel asked.

"An inexplicable mood. I feel fatality closing in on me."

"Tell your beads then," said Nigel rudely.

"Indeed, I could do worse. I remember, I took a terrible *miá* one time in Cork. It was the day they shot Kevin O'Higgins. I happened to be in a pub that evening when the news came through—he'd been killed on his way in to Mass. I'd felt desperate all day. And there it was."

"It must have been a great shock," Nigel said encouragingly.

"Oh, it was. A fella in the pub—we were all sitting around dumb as skates—I remember he upped at last and said, 'That was a terrible thing to do, a terrible thing. Sure why couldn't they have waited an hour and shot um when he came *out* of Mass?'"

Nigel broke into mirth. Chester asked, in a puzzled voice, "But I can't see why that would have been any better."

"God preserve me from the heathen! Absolution, boy, absolution. And may *your* sins be forgiven."

"I just don't see it," Chester persisted. "Are you telling me this O'Higgins would go to hell or something because he hadn't made his confession? Really, Charles, must you be so superstitious? If O'Higgins was a good man—had been—why should he be punished?"

"But who knows what crimes, what secret sins another man may have on his soul?" replied Charles somberly.

"Oh, nonsense!" Chester burst out, his black-gloved hands firm on the steering wheel. "Sorry, I did not mean to offend against your faith. And I suppose for all we know O'Higgins would have had a good many murders on his conscience."

"Murders?" Charles's voice was loud and deep as a stag's belling.

"Well, I mean—in the Troubles, you know—and then your Civil War."

With a titanic effort, Charles got himself under control. "Do you suggest that, when a soldier in a war for freedom kills an enemy it is murder?" he asked dangerously.

"Oh, was your Civil War a war of freedom? Freedom for whom? From what I've read, it was just a paying off of old scores." Chester's pugnacity quite startled Nigel, who said lightly,

"You must realize, Chester, the Irish held permanent shooting rights over the English."

Charles turned on him. "And why not? For three hundred years you English were a hostile garrison in my country. Will nothing get that into your thick heads? Though I'd rather have Cromwell or the Tans than high-minded bastards like Charles Wood or Trevelyan, who committed genocide in Ireland when the potato famine broke out—all for the sacred principle of Free Trade."

"But what's all *this* to do with your Civil War?" asked Chester.

"That was different. The country had to be settled. And I'm *told* you had a Civil War over here. *Do* you call the soldiers who fought in *that* war *murderers?*"

"All right, all right. I'll modify my statement." Chester shook his head. "O'Higgins must have had many *deaths* on his conscience. All right?"

"On his mind, not on his conscience. The Hierarchy approved the steps which the Free State government took to restore order."

"Which they did *not* do when the Sinn Fein rising took place in 1916," said Chester firmly. "The Church was against you then."

"So you've read some history. Ah, well, bishops are not infallible. But they came round. Do you remember Yeats's lines?—

> "An Abbot or Archbishop with an upraised hand
> Blessing the Tricolour. 'This is not,' I say,
> 'The dead Ireland of my youth, but an Ireland
> The poets have imagined, terrible and gay.'

"Yes, even Willie Yeats came round in the end."

Listening to them Nigel realized how much they had been on edge—all three of them. Why? Perhaps it was the mood of soldiers who are going back into the firing line after a leave. On the seat behind, Charles had audibly returned to the bottle; he did not attempt to offer it 'round. The instrument-panel light cast a faint glow on Chester's face, its features inscrutable. Nigel himself felt uneasy. All that talk about shooting and murders—how had the conversation taken so sinister a turn? And in the artificial light of head lamps and road lights, the built-up area as they approached the city—those extraordinary gas stations, eating houses, wooden shacks, kiosks, blaring bill-boards—took on a purely grotesque aspect, so that it seemed less the shoddy purlieus of a city than a fantasia of the unconscious.

And when they got out at the great gate of Hawthorne House, the Superintendent stopped Nigel. He handed him a piece of paper. It was a message from Lieutenant Brady, asking him to ring. Nigel went hurriedly up to his room.

"Lieutenant Brady, please. This is Nigel Strangeways, calling from Hawthorne House. . . . Hello, Brady, I'm just back from the country."

"I thought you'd like to know. We found the gun."

"You did? Where?"

"It was hidden among a stack of old cartons in the yard of one of the downtown cafés John Tate told us he'd visited."

Nigel was silent, dumfounded. Fantasy had caught up with him, turned into reality, and kicked him in the teeth.

"Can you hear me?" Brady asked.

"Yes, I heard you," said Nigel. "How do you know it's the gun? Got Tate's name embossed on it?"

"It's the same caliber as the murder weapon."

"So are several million other pistols. Fingerprints?"

"None. It's been cleaned, inside and out."

"How thoughtful of someone. And I must say John Tate was most considerate to tell you where to look for the weapon. I do like murderers who cooperate."

10 ☞ Confessions and Blackmail

The whole thing is preposterous, Nigel meditated as he shaved next morning. Quite meaningless—except to demonstrate the power of sheer coincidence. Young John Tate invents a story to account for his whereabouts after the murder and, lo and behold, the police find a gun of the right caliber in one of the cafés he invented visiting.

But is it meaningless, after all? I have only John's word, and Sukie's, that she had him hidden in her house *all the time*. He, or she, could have stepped out and stashed the gun in that downtown café: they wouldn't want it lying about in her own apartment block. That darned girl cannot be relied on to tell the truth for three minutes on end: and her lies, so far, have been in direct ratio to the disinterestedness of her motive for telling them.

Well, the test will be easy. They'll fire specimen bullets from the .25 automatic pistol they've found, and the markings on them will or will not be identical with those on the bullet which killed Josiah. Either way, it will not be necessary for me to confess to Brady about having found John in Sukie's house. "On a bullet we find the *sum total* of the peculiarities of the particular barrel," as Söderman and O'Connell eloquently put it: what trouble it would save if one could examine human peculiarities under a microscope.

A thought came to Nigel. He rang the Master's number, but it was May who answered.

"Zeke's just left. He's flying the shuttle to New York for a conference. I expect him back late this evening. Can I help you, Nigel? Are you there still?"

"Oh? Hm. Yes, May. Sorry. I just remembered something Zeke told me when I first came over."

"You sound very peculiar. Are you all right?"

"Fine, thanks. Except for feeling sore where I've just kicked myself."

Nigel rang off. He had an appointment with Brady at ten o'clock, which gave him time for breakfast and a visit to the Cabot Travel Bureau. Taking a taxi into the city, he then presented himself at Brady's precinct house.

"Looks like being another fine day," said the Lieutenant. He eyed Nigel in a calculating manner, as though deciding just where he should insert a stiletto.

"Have you identified the gun yet?" Nigel asked.

"Its numbers have been filed off. I should hear the result of the bullet tests any minute."

"Are you a betting man?"

"Why?"

"I'll lay you fifty to one that the gun you found didn't kill Josiah Ahlberg."

"Not taken. But you seem very sure of yourself, Mr. Strangeways."

"John Tate wouldn't have given you the name of that café if he'd killed Josiah and hidden the gun there. He's not that stupid."

Brady offered no comment. He took out a pack of Chesterfields and flipped one to Nigel across the desk.

"Any café proprietor, or customer even, would be likely to hide his gun when he heard the cops were nosing around the cafés in the district," Nigel went on.

"Sure, sure."

"You sound remarkably indifferent," said Nigel, somewhat exasperated.

Brady gave him one of his steeliest looks. "You did say that the Tates are not your clients, didn't you? Neither of them?"

"I'm interested in them. But they haven't hired me."

"That's tough on Miss Tate, maybe."

"Why?"

"You see, she's just confessed."

"Confessed? Sukie?" Nigel assumed she had confessed to sheltering her brother after the murder. Fortunately he did not make this apparent to Brady. "You must be out of your mind."

The Lieutenant took a folder of typewritten sheets from a drawer and placed it on the desk. Then explained that John Tate's lawyer happened to be visiting him the previous night when the searchers brought in the gun. Tate had disclaimed all knowledge of it; but the lawyer must have communicated the new information to Sukie, for she had come into the station early this morning and made a statement. "Here it is." Brady tapped the folder.

"But you can't take it seriously," Nigel protested. "You know what she's like—madly quixotic. She'll do anything to protect her brother."

"Okay, the dame's screwy; but I questioned her for a couple of hours, and she's got the whole story pat. Which is interesting as we monitored her interviews with him here: he told her nothing about his discovery of the body. Now, if she wasn't in touch with him between then and giving himself up, how in hell could she have got every last fact about the killing correct?"

"May I read it?" asked Nigel, playing for time.

"Sure."

It was certainly the most impressive confession Nigel had ever read. According to her statement, Sukie had worked out the murder plan with great care. Having made arrangements for John to be interviewed by Josiah at 10:30, she went to visit Josiah herself a few minutes before 10:00. She was wearing trousers, a heavy coat and a man's cap to conceal her hair: no one saw her, or at least no one recognized her, as she passed through the court. Josiah opened the door to her. She began to make an appeal to him on her brother's behalf: She was getting nowhere—she became desperate. When the Food Man started his hullabaloo, she moved behind the desk and shot Josiah in the temple. She went out again when the Food Man had moved on to the next entry, forgetting to lock the door, which Josiah must have left on the catch when he let her in.

The general sequence of events Sukie could have constructed by making inquiries from John's lawyer. But, rigorously questioned by Brady, she had given a precise description of the office, of Josiah's position at the desk, of the wound, of the body as it lay dead on the floor, of her horror when she remembered leaving the door unlocked, so that in due course her brother would walk in and be confronted by the corpse.

Sukie was equally precise about her motive. Hatred of Josiah for the way he had treated John, fear of his making public the episode with Charles Reilly, which he had threatened to do, weighting his evidence against her, unless she broke it off with Mark.

"Hmph," said Nigel, when he had perused the document this far. "Very pretty. But I suppose she ruined it all by saying she hid the gun in that café yard."

"No. She claims she chucked it over the Grant Bridge a couple of days later. A fine place to do it. The water's tidal there, and very deep, and the bottom's muddy, so there'd be little chance of recovering the gun."

"She goes up in my estimation every minute. Where does she say she *got* the gun, though?"

"A friend lent it to her when she was going on one of these peaceful pro-integration marches down South. She did not take it with her. And she refuses to give us the friend's name."

A plainclothes man came in and whispered to Brady. "You'd have won your bet, Mr. Strangeways. Result negative. That .25 did not fire the fatal shot." Brady fiddled with a paper knife on his desk. "I ask myself two things. *How* did she come by all this information if she didn't kill Ahlberg? Any ideas?"

"And the second thing?"

"Would any woman with a cute automatic pistol fire just the one bullet from it? Nah! She'd shut her eyes and spray the whole magazine into him. Or maybe not shut her eyes."

"So what are you going to do about Sukie?" asked Nigel.

"Let her cool off for a day or so, maybe."

"But you have no grounds for holding her."

"She's confessed, hasn't she?"

"I'd like to talk to her."

Brady gave Nigel an odd look. "But she refuses to talk to *you*. She particularly told me to block you off. She even put it in writing, in case you thought we'd been pressuring her." He handed Nigel a sheet of paper. "She's screwy. I told you."

Nigel did not trouble even to glance at the paper. "Well, that's fine. I'll send her some cookies."

It was Brady's turn to be disconcerted. "What the heck? Aren't you interested in what happens to her?"

"Extremely. For one thing, I want her to stay alive. She'll be safe enough in a prison cell."

"For God's sake! Don't tell me someone is gunning for *her*."

"No. But I'm expecting another murder attempt before long. If Sukie and John are enjoying the state's hospitality, at least they can't be accused of—"

"Hey! Are you serious?"

"Yes. And the only way to bring the criminal out into the open is to inform the press that you are detaining John and Sukie."

Lieutenant Brady lit another cigarette, with great deliberation. "Spell it out. I'm just a boneheaded cop."

It took Nigel the best part of half an hour to spell it out. Brady moved from incredulity to an astonished acceptance. "It *could* be," he said when Nigel had finished. "But can you handle your end?"

"I hope so. You'll have to risk that. If you pulled him in before we've made the necessary investigations, you-know-who would come down on you like a hydrogen bomb. Your case must be watertight."

"Don't I know it!"

They discussed ways and means. Nigel was certain he now knew the identities of the killer and his next victim: Brady was almost persuaded too. But how to frustrate X without putting him on his guard? It would take a little time to make the necessary investigations, and there was no certainty that their results would be positive enough to produce an open-and-shut case, and in this little time X would believe he had a free hand.

"I could put a police guard over him," said Brady.

"That would defeat the object of the exercise."

"Well, you have to get some sleep yourself—or don't you?"

"He'd never make the attempt in a conventional way. Therefore, no daggers or bombs, and not a gun again. He's extremely subtle."

"Sounds like you might run into danger yourself."

"Would you rather keep me safe and cozy in a cell here?" Nigel asked. "You could, you know."

Brady gazed at him, only half puzzled. "We seem to be getting a lot of confessions just now."

"Sukie *was* sheltering John. In her house. I found him there. I told him to give himself up. Forward with the handcuffs."

"I suspected this all along." Brady's tone was deep-freeze. "You

could have gotten yourself into serious trouble, Mr. Strangeways."

"But you need your agent at Hawthorne."

"You wasted my men's time, sending them chasing around
downtown. Just to keep the law off that crazy dame. At your
age, I guess— Oh, well, let it ride." The Lieutenant fastened
his eyes upon some invisible object on the ceiling. "On the side
table to your right, Mr. Strangeways, you may observe a box. It
welcomes contributions from the grateful public to our police-
benefit fund. The fund buys comforts for sick but deserving
cops."

"I never thought I'd find myself blackmailed in a police
station."

"We live and learn. If it would ease your mind," said Brady,
poker-faced still, "you could call it a fine."

"A fifty-dollar fine would perhaps be appropriate?" Nigel
stuffed some notes into the box.

"We are most grateful. Let me know what you find out at your
end." Brady grinned suddenly, like a sunburst. "And try to keep
out of trouble." . . .

"I tried to call you earlier," said Mark. "Twice. But you
seemed to be dug in on the telephone all afternoon."

"It was a transatlantic call. To Clare. We had rather a lot to
talk about."

"Who's Clare?"

"My girl. Clare Massinger. She's a sculptor."

It was 6:30 in the evening. The two were sitting over drinks
in Mark's room.

"Have a good day yesterday?" asked Mark.

"Very interesting."

"I'm sorry I couldn't come with you. I'd a date with Sukie.
The girl carries a torch for you—did you know that?"

"It'll burn out. By the way, have *you* heard from her today?"

"No. Should I have?" Mark paused. "She's not got into trouble, has she? Any more trouble, I mean?"

Nigel looked noncommittally at his companion. "She went to Brady this morning and made a statement. She said it was she who killed your brother."

Mark Ahlberg went rigid in the chair. His eyes, staring at Nigel, seemed unable to focus: his body began trembling. "But that's impossible, absurd." He spoke at last, in a whisper, as if trying out his voice after a period of solitary confinement.

"I'm sorry, Mark, but is it? I read the statement. It was plausible, to say the least. Her story was perfectly coherent and intelligible—Brady couldn't shake it, and the police have a built-in skepticism about confessions, they get so many bogus ones from crackpots during a murder case."

"Do *you* believe it?" asked Mark anxiously.

"The question is, whether Brady believes it. He's holding her anyway, on suspicion. It'll be in the papers tomorrow."

"But *why?*" Mark almost bleated it.

"Why did she murder him, or why did she confess?"

Mark brought his fist down on the table with appalling violence, cracking the wood. "*Confess,* you bloody goddam fool! *Why* did she confess?"

"To shield her brother? She feared they were going to charge him with the crime. She's a quixotic girl. Didn't you find her very worried yesterday?"

"No, not more than usual these last days. She's not been—well, very communicative."

Nigel gave him a long, ruminative gaze. "Or, of course, there could be another reason."

"What's that?"

"She might have done it for your sake," said Nigel.

"Mine?"

"She knew you were under grave suspicion too. Did she perhaps know more?"

Mark was picking his words deliberately now, as though he were walking through a minefield. "Know more? More about what? What are you trying to say?"

"More about your movements on the night of the crime."

Mark gave a jangled laugh. "Oh, for Chrissake! Are you suggesting I confessed to her I'd killed my brother, and in a noble way she decided to cover up for me? You've been reading too many women's magazines."

"Women can be insanely heroic in real life too. I know of a woman who persisted in giving her son an alibi though he'd raped and strangled a girl of ten, and she knew it."

"I don't call that heroic. Anyway, I'm not Sukie's son. If anyone is, it's John. And she wouldn't do anything so melodramatic for me." Mark gave Nigel a rueful look. "Hell, I need another drink after that. Shall I fix one for you?" He busied himself with the bottles. "Will they let me see her?"

"Ask Brady. She refuses to see me."

"Now why should that be?"

Nigel shrugged.

"You said it would be in tomorrow's papers?"

"It's probably in this evening's. But I don't think you take one."

Mark frowned. "What will happen to her? It's going to hold up her thesis, if it doesn't wreck it altogether. That's a damned shame—she's very promising, you know."

"She's got bigger worries than a thesis. And there's your own position to consider."

"Meaning?" Mark had gone tense again.

"What will your father do when he reads she's been arraigned for murder?"

"I see what you mean. It'll certainly give the old man a handle."

"His son engaged to a girl who's accused herself of murder?"

"That's all he needs. I guess he'll alter his will if I don't break it off with Sukie."

"And will you?"

"The ten-thousand-dollar question. Before this happened, I might have," said Mark slowly. "Sukie and I—well, it turned out we're not exactly the two halves of one egg. Twin hemispheres. She's beautiful, attractive, intelligent. I thought she was it—yet I've found I can't feel as close to her as maybe I should to marry her. But now I'd be a heel to throw her over." Mark gave Nigel a rather pathetic look, as if appealing for reassurance.

"It's quite a problem," Nigel agreed.

"What would you do?"

"Nothing at present. Wait to see what happens. It's about time *her* father turned up, isn't it?"

"I suppose," replied Mark indifferently. "But what could he do? They haven't been close for years, and he's a broken reed, or so Sukie claims. She might even refuse to see him."

There was a knock at the door. Mark rose and let in Chester, who carried a neatly folded evening newspaper. He looked indignant and pestered. "Have you seen this? It says Sukie has made a statement to the police. Is she mad?"

"Nigel's been telling me about it."

"Is this true?" Chester asked. "She's confessed? It can't be."

"Perfectly true," said Nigel.

"Nigel thinks—" began Mark.

"The statement was quite-voluntary. No pressure. Brady has checked it very conscientiously, so far as he can," Nigel interposed smoothly.

"But surely he has no evidence, outside this phony confession?

He's not going to charge her, is he?" Chester's voice went up into an angry squeak.

"Hey, take it easy, Chester," said Mark.

"He will need to get certain corroborative evidence first, I dare say." Nigel explained. "There *might* be conspiracy between Sukie and her brother. I simply don't know. But things don't look too good for them at the moment. The trouble is, she showed far more knowledge about the circumstances of the murder than she should have. Where could she have got it from, if she's innocent?"

"That certainly is peculiar," said Mark, looking up from the newspaper. "All this detail. I don't like it." He shivered.

"You *believe* it?" asked Chester accusingly.

"Now, now, calm down, old son, and fix yourself a drink."

"*Me* calm down! It passes my understanding how you can sit there and—"

"It won't help any, going into hysterics about this," said Mark coldly.

"Oh, crap! If you're not concerned about Sukie, I *am*. You're engaged to the girl—or maybe you've decided this is a nice out for you."

"Don't give me that, Chester!" said Mark formidably. "One Josiah was quite enough, preaching at me."

Nigel gazed quizzically at the two adult brothers quarreling like the boys they had once been, their academic skins cast aside. Of course, if the tiff was staged, it would support his theory of collaboration between them; but the theory no longer held any attraction for him. Deciding to bring them back to the point, Nigel broke in on their wrangle. "Listen. You both believe John and Sukie to be innocent. Right?"

The brothers nodded.

"Good. Well, if they are, there's a killer still stalking your academic grove. So be sure and lock your doors at night; and don't find yourselves alone with anyone—repeat, *anyone*—except a pupil of course; always have a third person present."

"You curdle my blood," said Mark, but less lightly than he intended.

"But why should anyone—why should he try to—to do anything to us?" Chester was gobbling a bit, and looking even more tense than usual.

"Because he *knows* John and Sukie are innocent, therefore knows her 'confession' is bogus, and therefore assumes the police will prove it false sooner or later and then will turn their attention back on the original suspects."

"Meaning me," said Mark.

"You and Chester."

"But they can't. They—they're s-satisfied with my alibi." Mark was almost stammering.

"You two had the strongest motives. If X felt called upon to take action again, his obvious move would be to liquidate one of you, make it look like suicide, forge a suicide note. Suspect kills himself, leaving confession."

"If this is the New Melodrama, you can have my ticket," said Mark.

"You're surely not serious?" asked Chester uneasily.

"Of course he's not. It's the British sense of humor. Very s-sick."

"I'm just warning you both," said Nigel equably. "If I'm the Cassandra of Hawthorne, it's not my funeral." . . .

May Edwardes, once again, put her finger on it. Nigel had gone later that night to tell the Master the recent developments. Neither of them could credit Sukie's "confession."

"I went to see John on Sunday," said Zeke. "He was in a bad way, I thought. He hasn't much stamina, poor fellow—and what he's got, he's wasting on self-pity. I'd guess it was his mental condition more than the finding of the gun that drove Sukie to make this quixotic gesture."

"I wonder what *he* thinks of it," said May. "Are they going to bring a charge against her?"

"All they could charge her with is being an accomplice after the fact. She sheltered her brother—this is not to go outside the room—after Josiah's death."

May's protuberant eyes fixed on Nigel incredulously. "But that's—I thought—"

"Yes, and it was you who put me onto where he was hiding. I told him he must give himself up."

"Well, then, we must get her out," said May briskly. "Zeke, you must go first thing tomorrow and bail her out. We can't have the poor girl incarcerated among a lot of crooks, tarts and perverts."

"Would they give permission?" asked Zeke uneasily.

"I should think so. With your surety. But I wouldn't try to bail out John too. We need him where he is."

"*Need* him?"

"Yes. I believe the murderer is nearer home, and Brady's now inclined to believe it too. And if we're right, the murderer's going to try again."

There was an appalled silence. Then May asked forthrightly, "Who?"

"Not one of—one of us here?" said the Master. "One of the Faculty?"

"I'm sorry. Yes."

Zeke's bony face looked agonized. "This will ruin Hawthorne," he muttered.

"Now don't be absurd, my dear," said May, trying to be soothing. "It's not your fault. Don't worry. It will all be forgotten in time."

"But how does this tie in with keeping John Tate in jail?" Zeke protested. "I don't see the connection."

Nigel's pale-blue eyes regarded him levelly. "The murderer is afraid of the police charging John with his own crime."

"But that's perfectly ridiculous!" exclaimed May. "Surely a scapegoat is just what he'd want?"

"Not in this case. He wants someone *else*—one particular person—to be accused. If John were accused, it would wreck the murderer's plans."

"Well, it's all beyond me."

"I don't know why you have to be so enigmatic, Nigel." May beat her fist impatiently on the sofa. "Who *is* this person you're talking about?"

"Now don't get mad, my dear. Nigel has always had a weakness for the cryptic."

"Well, he should try to control it," said May tartly. "All this talking in code! I only hope *you* can decode it."

The Master and Nigel were gazing at each other straightly. The Master gave him an almost imperceptible nod. Nigel said good night and left.

11 ☞ The Cup and the Lip

And why *had* he talked in that riddling
way? wondered Nigel as he walked toward the shops next morning. Why the reluctance to come out clear with his suspicions?
Could it be that in his own mind he had begun to hedge—that
the hard outlines of the case he had so confidently made to Brady
were becoming blurred? True, Zeke seemed to have taken the
point he'd been hinting at; and it was not desirable to set it out
for May in black and white—one could never be quite sure of
that unpredictable woman's reactions—she might jump the gun
in some way that would create embarrassment for Nigel.

He came to a main thoroughfare and crossed, still consciously
reminding himself that the traffic would hurl itself at him from
the left side first. He looked in at an antique shop window, hoping that something might take his eye which he could bring back
for Clare; but the articles on display seemed as mediocre as usual.
He was in a bad mood; he thought, these are the poshest shops
in Cabot, yet the jewelry they exhibit looks like the stuff a street
vendor drags out of an attaché case in Oxford Street. American
women are too busy bossing their husbands or trotting off to their
analysts' to have any time for developing taste. All these chunky
ornaments and depressing beads, t'chah! All right, I know I'm
being unfair. This is only a provincial city which happens to
possess a great university. Clare, I'm fed up with it, I want to
come home.

A yellow bus nearly put an end forever to Nigel's transportation problems as he started to cross the street again, against the red light. A traffic policeman high up in a sort of kiosk bawled at him. To escape the blast, he dived into a shop and bought a quantity of cookies. Outside, a group of girl students were licking at enormous chocolate ice-cream cones: the human tongue, Nigel thought, is not only an unruly member but a singularly unprepossessing one. Well, usually: Sukie's is like a cat's, neat and nice. And just lay off that, my boy!

It would be too soon to expect a return call from Clare today. He had told her he'd be near the telephone between 6 and 7 P.M., American time, every night till he heard from her. But she'd have to call in one of his friends at the Yard to make her investigations official; and none of these friends was exactly a man of leisure. In the meantime, Brady's men would be pursuing the new line of inquiries at this end. One could only wait.

Nigel went next to the famous tobacconist's shop opposite the oldest part of the university buildings. Here he ran into Charles Reilly, who was buying several packs of the Irish cigarettes which he had discovered the resourceful firm stocked.

"Hello there, Nigel."

Nigel made his purchase and they walked out into the street together. They paused for a moment to look at photographs of the Cabot football team displayed in the tobacconist's window.

"Did ye ever see the game?"

"Only on television. It's confusing."

"It's a great spectacle. Very fierce and intellectual. Like a bloodthirsty game of chess. I have a spare ticket for Saturday—they're playing Yale. Will you come with me?"

"Why, yes, I'd love to, Charles."

"I was going to take Sukie, but I hear she's in the clink."

"She may be out by Saturday," Nigel told him.

"So her confession's all cod? I knew it must be. It was an eejut thing to do."

"The Master's going to bail her out, I think. I don't know what the process involves over here."

"And what about her brother?"

"Ah, that's a different matter. He's not clear of suspicion yet. Far from it."

"So Sukie's great sacrifice was in vain."

They were walking, rather aimlessly, down a street which led to the river. Charles Reilly had the gait of a front-row forward— stocky, head down as if about to drive into the opposing scrum, slightly bandy-legged, arms held out a little from the sides, the fingers half clenched. A gorilla walk, thought Nigel; and he did not altogether care for Charles's last remark—there had been a touch of a jeer in it. Maybe Charles, thought Nigel, in the deplorable male way, still resented Sukie's not succumbing to his advances. Nigel's faint disapproval must have communicated itself to Charles's Irish intuition, for he said:

"Ah, but I'm sorry for the girl. She's not cut out to be a Joan of Arc. She needs a man, that one."

"She has one, hasn't she?" Nigel asked.

"Mark do you mean? I said 'a man.' Sure he's terrified of her."

"Terrified? That's pretty fierce."

"Oh, sure, he's fascinated by her, like a rabbit with a stoat. He dances to her tune all right, but he dislikes himself for doing it; so then he recoils from her and keeps a distance. He doesn't commit himself, because he's scared of her intensity, scared he is he'd burn up in it. He's like a great clever moth, that knows enough about the flame to stop plunging into it, however much it fascinates him."

"Well, now, that's very interesting, Charles."

They turned right, along the grassy slope by the river.

"You know, I'd have thought *she* might be a bit frightened of

Mark," Nigel continued. "That streak of wildness in him."

Charles's blue eyes, the color of the river in the sunlight, flashed at him brilliantly. "Oh, she's frightened of no man. Unless it's Chester."

"Chester?"

"It surprises you, doesn't it now? Well, Sukie told me once why she broke it off with him. It was the same thing that had first attracted her to him—a sort of cold, driving, undercover ambition. But then it began to alarm her because she felt he had it so thoroughly under control—you know, no boasting about his potentialities—just sort of a horrid, mad, wordless, armor-plated self-confidence, which peeked out at her occasionally from beneath that surface of his."

"That's an interesting viewpoint."

"It is that." Charles nodded. "She had a queer dream one night, she told me. The lass said she was in bed with Chester—in the dream, I mean—and suddenly he turned into some fancy kind of time bomb. It kept ticking away, and sure she knew it was going to go off sometime, but she couldn't get out of the bed and run away. She woke up at last, in a cold sweat. After that, says she, she lost her nerve and swapped Chester for Mark."

"And did Chester resent this?" Nigel asked. "Surely he must have."

"Well, now, I don't know. It was before I came over. Sukie says he went into his shell for a bit, and then came out again and then they got on all right in a real tepid sort of way. She doubts it meant all that much to him, and perhaps she's right. Well, I must go back. I've got that Brady coming to see me at eleven. Would you know what he wants?"

"To talk to you about the Sukie-Josiah-you complex, I imagine," Nigel said.

"Scraping the bottom of the barrel, eh? I wish the fella'd leave me alone. Oh, by the way, Nigel, I clean forgot, talking of Chester. Seems the chap's having a bit of a party in his room tonight—half nine about. And he wants you to come." . . .

Nigel was getting fidgety. Impossible to concentrate on the work for which he had come to Cabot. As for the investigation, it had now moved on from theory to practice, and the practical side must be left to the police—dull, slogging work which he nevertheless envied them. If the evidence they now sought were found, it would probably be found quickly and the case—so far as Nigel was concerned—would fizzle out. It would not have been necessary to drive the murderer into the open, with all the deadly dangers this implied. It became evident to Nigel that Brady had not taken very seriously the likelihood of a second attempt by the murderer, although he was impressed by Nigel's theory about the first one. And there was no doubt that Brady, with Papa Ahlberg on his tail, had not pursued one line of investigation nearly far enough last week.

Anyway, the battle had now moved to an area where Brady's men must infallibly either prove a murderer's guilt or establish a suspect's innocence.

Nigel watched two students run across the court carrying squash rackets, saw a window on the far side of the court opened and Mark's head poked out: Mark stayed thus a minute or two, engaged in what Nigel interpreted as deep-breathing exercises, then closed the window again. A turbojet passed over, fairly low: Nigel wondered idly if it was on the shuttle service between the city airport and LaGuardia. A gramophone on the floor above was playing *La Mer*. On Nigel's desk lay a slip of paper which had been pushed under his door before lunch—Chester's invitation to the little party that evening.

Nigel began to think again about the curious revelations

Charles Reilly had made that morning. Even allowing for Charles's usual poeticisms and hyperbole, they cast a strangely angled light upon the persons concerned—including Charles himself. Was it not odd that Sukie should have given Charles such intimate confidences? Was it after or before Josiah's discovery of them in a compromising position that she had done so? But of course, Nigel realized, Sukie's behavior could be boiled down simply to a girl's gratification at adding to her collection the scalp of a distinguished Irish poet. And that of a distinguished private eye from England?

He read till 7 P.M. No telephone call from Clare. So he walked to the nearest taxi stand three minutes away, had himself conveyed to an Italian restaurant in the suburbs, and ordered lasagne, a bottle of Bardolino, and a chocolate ice cream. He had discovered on a previous visit there that a chocolate ice, consumed with Bardolino, imparted to the latter a delicious flavor of wild strawberries. This bizarre discovery, passed on to friends at Hawthorne, had resulted in a sizable accession to the restaurant's clientele and to VIP treatment for Nigel from the proprietress.

Lingering over the meal, he suddenly realized it was well past nine. The wine, and the warmth of the restaurant, had made him sleepy. He paid his check, and decided to clear his head by walking back to Hawthorne.

When Nigel arrived at Chester's room, it was 9:40. Mark was there already, and Charles Reilly, and the Senior Tutor, together with two Faculty members from another House. Master Edwardes might stop by later, Chester told Nigel.

The room was desperately hot. A log fire burned in the grate, and presumably the central heating was on too. Charles, Mark and one of the strangers had already taken off their coats. Chester kept his on, looking spruce but anxious.

"I would like you to know Paul Andreyevsky and Mark Blair,"

Chester said as the strangers came over. "Colleagues of mine in the Business School."

Andreyevsky, Nigel noticed, in his manner of speech and appearance bore a strong resemblance to Chester. The two men shook hands with Nigel, announcing their names loud and clear.

"Paul Andreyevsky. I am most happy to meet you."

"Martin Blair. Nice to know you."

"Martin. Of course. I must apologize for a slip of the tongue," said Chester in some confusion. "Cheese? Bourbon? Something?" he offered Nigel. Chester has an owlish look, thought Nigel, accepting a cheese cracker and a drink: must be a bit pissed already: first time I've seen him like this. Nerves? But then, when one is a bit loaded oneself, it has the peculiar effect of making everyone else seem drunk.

Nigel stated this proposition to Blair and Andreyevsky, who received it politely and began to ask him about his reactions to the United States and Cabot.

"Entirely favorable," answered Nigel, with a large gesture which nearly swept the bourbon off the table beside him. "A great country. A great university. Highest standards of learning, intelligence and manners. And what other nation provides toasted corn muffins for breakfast?"

"It's very, very gratifying to have you say so," said Andreyevsky.

"Not at all, Paul, if I may call you Paul. I fear that is not an euphonious sentence, but it speaks from the heart. I would now like to enlarge upon my approbation for the American Way of Life." Nigel did so for some little time, far from daunted by the knowledge that he was now the center of attention. "If I have any criticism to make," he was concluding, "it is of your failure to provide a National Health Service. Surely—"

"But our medical science is the finest in the world," protested Martin Blair.

"You can't be talking about those butchers over the road," Mark began.

"Now now, Mark, that's no way to talk about the Cabot Medical Faculty." Zeke Edwardes had come in, unobtrusively as ever. With his entrance the party broke up and re-formed. Everyone seemed to be jockeying for a position farther from the fire.

"D'you know, the American Way of Life," announced Charles Reilly when they seemed to have settled down slightly, "brings me out in a sweat. What with your brinkmanship and your central heating—I say, do you *never* open a window, Chester?"

Mark, who had been looking rather anxiously at his brother who had slumped on a sofa, went over and opened a window an inch.

"Everything's so hot. To say nothing of being grilled by the police this morning," Charles went on.

"Oh, Charles, for God's sake, can't we forget it for an hour or two?" Chester looked up. His face was desperate, or despairing—Nigel could not make out which, though the difference, he felt, was important.

"Yes, we should!" said the Master. "We have other troubles, such as this row over the General Education proposals."

Andreyevsky and Blair looked slightly shocked at that. The Master, Nigel realized, had had an unfortunate relapse into the old Oxford manner. However, the company in general welcomed his diversion as a way out of an embarrassing subject, and soon several of them were launched on the General Education controversy. Under cover of their discussion, Nigel moved over to the corner of the window where Charles Reilly sat, mopping his red face.

"Brady gave you a bad time?"

"Bad time, is it? He put me through the mangle. And he a fellow Irishman too!" muttered Charles. "Made me try to remember all my movements for days after the murder. As if I could! As if it was of the least importance. Obviously he need only have been concerned with the one night."

"Why?"

"Because if I'd shot the fella, I would have gone out to get rid of the gun as soon as possible. How could I have known John Tate would come along and hide the body for me, so that I could have several days' grace? And anyway," said Charles with an impish look, "I haven't got a gun. I gave up the dreadful things thirty years ago."

"So then?" asked Nigel.

"So then the fella raked up all the little episode you know of. Had not Josiah threatened to expose it? And he had not. Did Sukie ever tell me he'd tried it on with her? She did not. On and on and on. They certainly earn their salaries. Of course he was waiting for me to contradict myself. Discrepancies in my evidence! Too bad I couldn't supply him with any." Charles sighed. "You know, Nigel, Josiah was a man without generosity: but he was no blackmailer, it wasn't in his nature." Charles sighed again, and swiveled a blue eye at Chester. "Lookit, over there, the little fella has drink taken? Will you look at him?"

Chester was still lolling on the sofa at the other side of the room, his face white and perspiring, paying little heed to the academic controversy raging around him. Somebody asked him a question, to which he only grunted a monosyllabic reply. Just then Mark moved to his brother with obvious solicitude, and spoke a word in his ear: Chester, eyes shut, shook his head; he looked like a man waiting for news, who cannot abide any interruption of his expectant state of mind.

Nigel watched for a moment, then thoughtfully retired to the bathroom. Inquisitive as ever, he poked about. It was a small room, and it too was stiflingly hot. A shower behind a curtain; a basin, a mirror, the lavatory bowl: a sumptuous Turkish bath towel was the only article there different from the stock Hawthorne issue. Nigel opened the medicine cupboard above the washbasin. It was crammed with bottles and boxes of all sizes. One might have known Chester was a hypochondriac. There were palliatives against wind, for instance, influenza cure, sleeping pills, sedative and stimulant drugs, pile ointment, iodine, cough mixture, bandages, adhesive tape, two thermometers, a bottles of tables labeled "Phenergan," a plastic bottle of Gly-Oxide and a large bottle of some sort of cleaning fluid. Nigel stopped a general search and looked for Disprin, but could not find any: instead, he thoughtfully dissolved two tablets of Alka-Seltzer and drank them from the tooth tumbler, to take the edge off the hangover which was no doubt impending.

Returning finally, he found his hypochondriac host in a state of febrile aggressiveness. He was by then, of all things, giving the company a blow-by-blow account of the practical jokes he had suffered from. His speech was slurred, but the gravamen of his complaint was clearly directed against the Master and the Senior Tutor: in a properly disciplined community, he was saying, that sort of outrage could never happen. The two visiting instructors were highly embarrassed, the Senior Tutor more sardonic than ever. Zeke Edwardes was listening to the tirade with his usual courteousness.

"The first thing students should learn is to respect authority," Chester was saying. "Do you or do you not agree, Senior Tutor?"

"The first thing they should learn is to grow up. And that does not apply to students only," was the acrid reply. "Growing up means coming to see things in proportion."

"Now you talk just like my late lamented brother Josiah. Are you suggesting that I—?"

"I say take it easy, Chester," said Zeke. "Growing up is finding the limits of freedom—personal freedom—and balancing it against the rightful demands of the community. There are bound to be casualties on the way."

"And *I* have to be the casualty?" asked Chester angrily.

"Oh, now, wait a minute. Our men are young still: boys. The young have no sense of the adult community—why should they? They form gangs, splinter groups; but these are only a projection of the young man's ego. We hope that *unconsciously,* while they are here, they absorb the air of freedom, so that later they find themselves sitting easily to it, not exploiting it. You can't *discipline* them into accepting the right idea of freedom, any more than you can force them into understanding the nature of true society."

"So *you* would allow any measure of license," said Chester contumaciously, "as a—a sort of trampoline from which they can spring higher and higher and higher into the pure air of liberty?"

"No, no. My policy is to give them, subject to the necessary parietal rules, a little more freedom than at first they can adapt themselves to. I see it as a bait for them, rather than a way of life. Treat an adolescent as an adult, and with any luck he'll grow up quicker. I think it works. Don't you agree, Mark?"

"Well, I guess you're right, Master. But, Chester, I don't know why you're beefing about the *young;* I thought you thought *I*'d played these practical jokes on you."

It was the most embarrassing moment so far. Though Mark had spoken lightly, the rest averted their eyes from him to his brother.

But Chester appeared to have exhausted his brief spurt of animation. He muttered, *"Don*'t be absurd, Mark," in a rather shamefaced way, then relapsed into silence. Mark gave him a puzzled, anxious glance.

"Maybe we could all use some black coffee. Shall I make it, Chester?"

His brother nodded. The company, relieved, began to talk again. Nigel unobtrusively followed Mark into Chester's bedroom, where an electric kettle, an earthenware jug, and some large cups were already set out on a table. Mark grinned at him. "Hi. Things do get het up. Have you come to see I don't put poison in old Chester's cup?"

"Yes." Nigel smiled back.

Mark paused a moment in spooning out instant coffee into the jug and then proceeded. *"Toujours le phlegm anglais, hein?* Poor old Chester's in a queer state of mind tonight, don't you think? You know, I've never seen him loaded like this. If I'd been Master Edwardes, I'd have got mad at him."

"He was rather provocative, I must say."

"Oh, sorry, I forgot, you don't like cream. I'll boil you up some milk."

"Don't bother," Nigel protested.

But Mark was opening a carton and pouring the contents into a saucepan. Presently they returned to the sitting room. Mark put the tray on a side table for a moment, then carried it round to each of the guests in turn. Nigel, who was talking with Charles Reilly, poured himself a cup and added a little hot milk to it: Charles did the same. Mark finally came to Chester. The two visiting instructors were standing in front of the sofa, between Nigel and the Ahlberg brothers, so he did not get a view of the little *contretemps.* He only heard Chester exclaim, "Oh, damn you, you've spilt it *all* over my jacket!" and the noise of the coffee pot hitting the carpet.

"I'm terribly sorry, Chester, you jogged my arm though."

"No, *you* did."

Chester rose from the sofa and stood swaying, gazing in owlish consternation at his jacket, which was soaked with coffee: some of the hot milk had spilled over it too; the saucepan had fallen onto its side on the tray.

"Look, you've ruined it," Chester mumbled.

Mark was dabbing at his brother's lapels with a handkerchief. The others crowded round.

"That's no good. You'll never get the stain of hot milk out like that," said the Senior Tutor. "It needs cleaning fluid."

"Do you have some, Chester?" asked Mark. "Come along, we'll look."

He supported his brother toward the bathroom. Nigel followed. Mark had found the bottle of cleaning fluid and a large white handkerchief, and scrubbed vigorously at the lapels and chest of his brother's jacket. Chester was slumped on the lavatory seat, looking very drunk. Mark had to hold him with one hand or he would have fallen off. The little room was airless and steamy-hot.

"There, that should do it," Mark said at last. "Now put on another jacket, and come and be sociable again. Hey, buck up, Chester!" He turned to Nigel. "He's practically passed out."

Chester's face was greenish-white and sweating, his eyes closed. He tried to stand up. "Sorry, I feel so giddy."

"We'd best put him to bed, Nigel, don't you think?"

They half carried Chester into the bedroom, took off his jacket, trousers and shoes, and laid him on the bed. Then Mark solicitously pulled a blanket over him, and they went back to the sitting room.

"Chester's passed out. We've left him to sleep it off."

"He was certainly hitting it up with the liquor tonight," said the Senior Tutor.

"Well, it was a great party while it lasted," said Martin Blair.

The Master gave Nigel an indecipherable look, raising his eyebrows questioningly.

"I'm sorry Chester got so tough, Master," said Mark. "Too much alcoholic content, I'm afraid."

"Think no more of it," Zeke protested. "But I must be saying good night."

The other guests took their cue from him. Nigel left last, with Mark and Charles Reilly.

"He'll have a whale of a hangover tomorrow," said Charles.

"I can't think how I could be so clumsy," Mark commented. "I must be a bit pissed myself. I thought it was Chester who knocked the tray, just as I was going to pour him the coffee. He is accident-prone, poor old boy." . . .

Nigel let himself into his apartment, but did not go to bed. He was feeling far from sober himself, but sensible enough to realize that Chester, in his present condition, would be defenseless against anyone who wanted to do him harm. Though it was probably making Everest out of a molehill, precautions must be taken. Nigel would go out in five minutes' time, borrow the spare key from the Superintendent's office, get into Chester's apartment, and spend the night there on guard, ensuring that no one went in—or out.

At this point Nigel fell asleep.

He was awakened by his telephone bell ringing. An almost unrecognizable voice croaked at him. "Feel dreadfully ill. . . . Come quick . . . Poisoned . . . Quick . . . Help."

12 ☞ "Yesterday Is Mystery"

Some eight hours later Nigel was sitting in his own room again, trying to make some sense of an event which had run so counter to his cherished theory of all that had previously occurred in Hawthorne House.

In response to the phone call Nigel had rushed to Chester's apartment and had found him there in a semicomatose condition. Nigel had rung for a doctor, whose name he found in Chester's address book, and had waited. The doctor had come, had examined Chester, kept his conclusions to himself, and sent for an ambulance. Chester was now in the Cabot Infirmary—still, so far as Nigel knew, alive.

There was little else he could congratulate himself on. He had been asleep for less than an hour that night when the telephone had rung; but that hour would have been plenty of time for a killer to have entered Chester's room and to have poisoned the defenseless man. If that was the way it was done. The bottles, cups and glasses from the party had still been there, of course, when Nigel arrived. Brady, who had come right after the ambulance, had taken them all away for chemical analysis of what was left in them, and taken the coffee pot, the saucepan, and Chester's jacket, for the same purpose.

"So your hunch was right," the Lieutenant had said sourly when there was time for a chat. "You just picked the wrong victim."

"So it seems."

"All that spiel about giving him rope. I guess I gave *you* too much."

"Well, it's saved you from arresting the wrong man. For a second time," said Nigel.

Whatever was the vehicle of the poison, Nigel was thinking now, it could not be the liquor they had all consumed: Chester had punctiliously poured it for his guests. Nor the coffee, the cream or the hot milk, for each of them had taken some without ill effects, while Chester's had been spilled over him before he could drink any. If X had introduced something—some barbiturate, say—into Chester's tumbler, it would surely be in such great quantity, to produce so drastic an effect, that he could not have failed to notice it before he refilled his glass. And if Chester was the victim, not the murderer, X should be Mark—of whom Nigel had told Chester to be wary.

But Mark might have gone back to Chester's rooms, while Nigel was asleep, and somehow poisoned his unconscious brother It was a *grand guignol* thought which Nigel shied away from.

Nigel shook his head. It was bewildering. Chester had croaked over the telephone "poisoned." This was odd in itself. A man who came briefly to consciousness out of a drunken stupor would surely ascribe his symptoms merely to the drink; particularly if he had never drunk so much before. Of course, Chester was highly sensitive to his physical condition, as the contents of his medicine cupboard so evidently showed: and he *had* been warned; and he *had* been poisoned.

Was he, last night, intuitively expecting some such attempt on his life? There had been that desperate look on his face now and then—the look of some creature that stands at bay: and the alternation of truculence with a kind of sodden lethargy.

Or, again, might not the "poisoning" have been purely accidental? With all those drugs in his bathroom, Chester could easily have dosed himself before the party with some drug (stimulant? sedative?) which became lethal if too much alcohol were poured on top of it. That happened fairly often even though it would seem that every American pill-taker had been warned about the liquor-barbiturate danger.

They would be checking on possibilities at the hospital. *Was* it accident? Suicide?

Nigel was looking out over the court. Down below, even at this early hour, a man was at work. He had spread a huge sheet over the grass, and was now trundling round it what appeared to be a vacuum cleaner in reverse: instead of sucking in the multitude of fallen leaves, it was blowing them onto the sheet. What a splendid, elementary invention, thought Nigel, who had suffered all too often in the past from the leaves which littered his Greenwich garden in autumn and had to be removed between two pieces of wood.

Then his body grew tense in the chair. Why *not* suicide? I've been assuming murder: but why not violence *in reverse* this time? The desperation on Chester's face last night—easily interpreted as the look of a man who has decided to put an end to himself: desperation and a touch of recklessness as well. And, when he rang me and said he'd been poisoned—that was the crisis so many would-be suicides undergo, when they see Death in close-up and wish they had not beckoned to him; and when a flicker of pride prevents their confessing what they have done. Instead, the man projects his violent impulse onto an imaginary other. A classical example of the schizoid process.

But *why* should Chester have set out to kill himself? The only possible motive is that he killed Josiah and knew Brady and I were close on his heels. He must have perceived that I had drawn the correct inference from that slip he had made on the journey to Concord. And when I warned the two brothers to be on guard against an attack, he would assume that it was Mark I warned against *him*. Perhaps he had even got wind of Brady's latest investigations. Anyway, he felt he'd run his course, been driven into a blind alley with high walls on either side.

Of course there's no proof. It'll all depend on what the policeman sitting beside Chester's bed may hear. And did he leave a suicide note? Brady examined his rooms very carefully, but does not seem to have found one.

Nigel stretched wearily. He went out for breakfast; then, returning, lay down on the sofa and slept for four hours. . . .

At five past six that evening his telephone bell rang again. It was Clare, speaking from London. He put pencil and paper in readiness beside him. She talked for five minutes: Nigel took a few notes, and asked a few questions.

"So I'm afraid it's pretty inconclusive," she ended. "But I hope it helps some. You do get into things. And I miss you. When are you coming home, darling?"

"In a few days, I hope. And thank you for trying. It needn't have been a waste of time. We've had a most dramatic night. Chester tried to kill himself."

"*Did* he now?"

"Yes. Damn! Someone's at the door. I love you. 'By."

Nigel opened the door, and Lieutenant Brady strode in. Nigel sat him down with a drink. "How is he?"

"They've pulled him through. I thought I heard you talking to someone just now?"

"That was Clare. From London."

"Oh, yeah? From *London?* Uh-huh." However, Brady did not sound madly interested.

But Nigel plowed ahead. "She got our friend, Chief Inspector

Wright, to have inquiries made at the airport hotel where Chester checked in. They bore out his statement to you, more or less. He arrived when he said he did, early on the Thursday morning. Registered. Told the receptionist he was going to put the 'do not disturb' notice on his door and sleep round the clock. For all we can prove, he did just that. Our people found no one who noticed him leaving the hotel shortly after he arrived—but it's a busy foyer, people coming and going all the time, and Londoners are totally unobservant anyway. On the other hand, there's no record of his having taken a meal in the hotel, either that night or the next morning. Which is more than a little odd."

"And no one noticed him entering the hotel on the Friday morning with a reeking revolver?" asked Brady.

"Strangely enough, no. The housemaid went into his bedroom about eleven on Friday. The bed appeared to have been slept in. His clothes were lying about. She assumed, quite naturally, that he'd forgotten to take the notice off the door when he went out."

"Well, it seems to sew up that end okay. He might have flown back to the States, killed Josiah, and returned to Britain, all within twenty-four hours. Or he might not. Big deal."

"What about your end?" asked Nigel.

"Not much more conclusive. He *could* have flown back to New York on the Thursday, taken the shuttle plane here, killed Josiah, shuttled back to New York, and caught a plane getting him to London in time to attend his first conference. Your point about his 'losing' the passport was a good one. We'd have been bound to examine it, and seen that it was stamped *twice* by the British authorities. Time-wise, the thing was just possible—we've checked it very carefully, though the schedule would be tight for the return via New York. He shoots Josiah at 10 P.M., takes a taxi to the airport, catches the 10:30 shuttle to New York, arrives at 11:30, boards the transatlantic plane which leaves at ten after midnight. He'd be taking a big risk: any delay along the line would wreck his schedule. Still, *in theory* it was possible."

"But your chaps have found no evidence of it?"

"Nobody who will swear to identification. They found a taxi driver who took up a fare from the stand in the Square at approximately 10:05 and brought him to the airport. He says the man was a bit out of breath, about the right size physically, but he didn't particularly notice his face. Same with the hostess on the shuttle planes he could have caught: we showed them the photographs of Chester: one of the girls *thought* he might have been on her ship, but she didn't pay him any attention apart from selling him a ticket."

"You'll have an identity parade, though, in due course?"

Brady gave Nigel an unfathomable look. "Sure. Yeah, we could do that thing."

"Papa Ahlberg permitting?"

Brady ignored the provocation. "The problem is the transatlantic flights. The shuttle ones are as impersonal as a ride in a crowded subway. But when you fly the Atlantic, you get more personal attention. We've questioned very closely the steward and hostesses who were on the one midnight flight from New York he could have taken. None of them appears to have recognized Chester as one of their passengers."

"He could have put on some rudimentary disguise."

"I'll give you that. And there was one guy who put his hat over his face and slept all the way through till they woke him with a breakfast tray."

"Chester told me he could never sleep on a plane. Did this fellow have a beard or something?"

"A mustache. We painted a mustache on a photo of Chester. One stewardess thought it *might* be—no, she couldn't swear to it—she'd seen hundreds of passengers since then—and this guy, she seemed to remember, had his face averted when the tray was passed to him."

"I see. Of course, Chester comes two-a-penny. He's a type of the American businessman. What about the baggage?"

"Baggage?"

"Chester'd left his things in the London hotel. Wouldn't a fellow flying the Atlantic without any baggage arouse some comment?"

"I'll inquire about that." Brady made a note. "But where you fall down, Mr. Strangeways, is the passenger lists. It'd be okay for him with the shuttle flights—you don't book for them. But you must have a reservation for a transatlantic flight. And Chester Ahlberg's name does not appear on the passenger list of any transatlantic plane he could have taken."

"What's to stop him booking a reservation under a false name?"

"It'd be checked against his passport."

"Are you sure? When he buys the ticket, you mean?"

"It should be," said Brady uneasily. "Anyway, it'd be checked against the passenger list by the immigration authorities, on both sides."

Nigel was silent for a few moments. "Suppose he'd 'borrowed' a friend's passport. Paid for the reservation in cash—in some other city—New York, maybe—so there'd be no question about the wrong name on a check. Chester's a very common American type, so the passport photograph could fit him reasonably well at a glance—the authorities don't pore over these photos. Yes," said Nigel, warming to his work, "he pinches a friend's passport; he'd only have to keep it for six days—oh, and perhaps a brief period beforehand when he bought the reservations. He flies to London under his own passport, uses the friend's for the trips to and from New York, then flies back to the city airport here four days later under his own passport again."

Brady gave him a humoring look. "So why, for God's sake, if

his own passport was not stamped twice in London, does he have to burn it?"

"That *was* my theory. He could just have lost it, as he said he did."

Nigel was too much preoccupied with the elegance of his new theorizing to notice the smile gathering at the corners of Brady's mouth.

"It's very, very ingenious, Mr. Strangeways. You must be a humdinger at building card-houses. So how do we prove it?"

"That's simple. You look again at the passenger lists for that Thursday. If you find the same name on a morning flight from London to New York and the midnight plane from New York to London, you'll know that's the name and passport under which Chester traveled."

"Um-m. You may have something there," Brady admitted. "*If* we found any such things."

"I'm surprised it didn't make you sit up and take notice. It must be fairly uncommon for anyone to do the round trip within a period of twenty-four hours."

"Oh, I don't know so much about that. There's a New York guy who regularly flies to bloodstock sales in Dublin, has dinner in Paris, and is back in his office creating hell next morning."

Lieutenant Brady took a sip from his glass, leaned back, and put his hands on his stocky thighs. Nigel glanced at him suspiciously.

"You're holding out on me, Brady. I don't like that innocent gleam in your eye."

"I guess I enjoy seeing a mastermind at work."

"Oh, come off it."

"I wouldn't like you to think I've been kidding you along all this time. But things have been happening today." Brady had an expression which on a less extravert face would be called "dreamy." "Yes, sir. First, we had all those glasses and cups from Chester's room tested. Result, negative. So how was it conveyed to him—whatever produced the coma?"

"He conveyed it to himself, before the party."

"Come again." Brady's green eyes had opened wide. Nigel outlined his theory of attempted suicide.

"You certainly do have your teeth fast in Chester Ahlberg. So he tried to kill himself because he believed we'd caught up with him?"

"That's the idea," Nigel said.

"Uh-huh. Well, now, as I was saying, I couldn't figure out how the poison was administered. And then I—I sort of got the smell of something. Remembering that jacket."

"Jacket?"

"Sure. The one he was wearing—we took it away for examination," Brady explained.

"Well, it was cleaning fluid, not prussic acid. I was there when Mark rubbed his brother down with it."

"So I had a talk with Rivers—he's the best pathologist in the state. He told me it had been discovered that, under certain conditions, the carbon tetrachloride given off by cleaning fluids can be dangerous. It can produce cirrhosis of the liver or kidneys—damage to the cells. They are not sure yet whether the carbon tetrachloride has a direct effect on these cells or works on them through its effect on the bloodstream. I had him ring the Infirmary. He asked about the symptoms. Greenish-white face, giddiness—you noticed that?"

"Yes."

"And another thing. When they'd pulled Chester 'round, he told the Infirmary doctors that it'd been 'like bells ringing in my head, louder and louder, the last one a dreadful clang.' "

"Good Lord!" Nigel exclaimed.

"Another symptom of carbon-tetrachloride poisoning, apparently."

"You said 'under certain conditions.' "

"Yep. A large intake of liquor would be likely to aggravate the poison's effect. And a hot, confined space is necessary if the fumes are to do their work."

"Chester's bathroom."

"Exactly."

"So," said Nigel after a pause, "it was accident."

"It *could* be accident."

"What d'you mean by that?"

"Or it could have been rigged to look like accident. By Mark Ahlberg."

"I suppose so."

"You told me Mark spilled the coffee and milk over Chester."

"I told you Chester *said* he did. Mark's line was that Chester tipped the tray himself."

"It would have to be Mark's line."

"Well, I don't know. It does seem to me a chancy way of trying to murder someone. Have there been any *fatal* cases of poisoning by carbon tetrachloride?"

"Yes. Rivers knows of them. Though the toxicity took between ten and fourteen days to kill. This one was near enough fatal, I guess. And don't forget, Mark knew he was still under grave suspicion for the murder of Josiah. He had to think up something for Chester that would look like accident."

"Or suicide," Nigel murmured.

"Sure. But if he'd intended it to be taken for suicide, he'd have faked up a suicide note."

Nigel began prowling round the room. He was disagreeably convinced by Brady's reading of events. The mawkish, basset hound cutout on the mantelpiece caught his eye. "I've grown to hate this damned dog," he exclaimed, and hurled it into the wastepaper basket. "You're going to charge Mark?"

"Looks like it."

"But the layman surely doesn't know about this cleaning-fluid danger."

"Very few laymen." Brady was poker-faced. "But after I'd had the talk with Rivers, I came back and did further checking. I found a copy of a medical journal with a page corner turned down at an article carrying an account of experiments on rats with carbon tetrachloride, and pointing out its danger. It was at the bottom of a pile of magazines in his cupboard."

"Mark's."

"No, Chester's."

Nigel was startled. "But that looks like suicide again."

"Perhaps Mark planted it there to make it look like suicide."

"The redhead in reverse," Nigel muttered obscurely. "He tried to plant *that* idea on us, yet he forgot to fake a suicide note? It doesn't sound very efficient."

"Well, I have an idea about that. Suppose he was going to return to Chester's room when everyone had cleared out, and plant a fake note some place—in a desk, maybe. But he went to sleep instead."

"Like me. What on earth do you—? Oh, I see. I *see. He'd* been affected by the fumes too? How simple. Congratulations, Brady. I think you must be right all along the line. The pattern is strangely neat too. Mark tries to go back to Josiah's room after shooting him. Mark means to go back to Chester's after poisoning *him*. In either case, something prevents it. Very pretty. Very symmetrical. Very tidy. Well, then this lets me out, and I can depart for England in peace."

"Hold it, Mr. Strangeways! The Homicide Department is greatly appreciative of your cooperation"—Brady put the phrase in sardonic quotes—"but we should like a few more chores from you." The Lieutenant described them. "We've a great deal of detail ourselves to work over before we have the case against Mark Ahlberg sewed up." He rose to take his leave. At the door he turned and said with a flashing grin, "Oh, I guess I forgot. Your girl friend would like a talk with you."

"My *girl* friend?"

"Miss Susannah Tate. We've released her."

"She is *not* my girl friend."

"Is that so? Well, I gather you're her father figure. Be seeing you." . . .

So the Master had been as good as his word, and gone bail for Sukie. What would happen to her brother, Nigel still did not know: he disliked the idea of that intelligent if unreliable young man being held in prison indefinitely, but there was nothing he could do about it. It was a high price to pay for a temporary loss of nerve. But at least there could now be no question of John, or Sukie, having had anything to do with the murder of Josiah: that, and the attempt on Chester, must have been one man's work; and who could the one be except Mark?

And if Mark had thought up this bizarre method of poisoning Chester, it must surely have been he who had thought up the no less bizarre practical-joke campaign. But why? Nigel bent his mind to it as he dug into Wiener schnitzel at a nearby restaurant. One had to revise all one's feelings about Mark and think of him as an essentially malicious character; or else find some rational link between the jokes and the poisoning. Malicious acts, for their own sake, were totally foreign to anything Nigel knew about Mark's nature: he never indulged even in the malice with which academic conversation is so liberally spiced. Well, then, what were the practical jokes meant to do to Chester or convey to the police? Drive him into real paranoia? One brother murdered and the other put away in a madhouse? A clear road to

Father Ahlberg's millions? Then why not persevere with the practical jokes? Wait a minute, though: the cleaning-fluid episode might be, not an attempt at murder, but the climax of this joke campaign—to give Chester the impression of some mysterious, implacable hostility always lying in wait for him.

Nigel paid his check and returned to Hawthorne House. Zeke and May were in their drawing room when he went over.

"You're looking tired, Nigel," May said sympathetically.

"Didn't get enough sleep last night. And I'm afraid I'm the bearer of evil tidings."

"But they said Chester would be all right. Zeke called to inquire this afternoon."

"It's about Mark. Lieutenant Brady is convinced he tried to kill Chester."

"The man must be mad," exclaimed May tartly.

Zeke had closed his eyes, as if he foresaw the blow. He suddenly looked his age, and more: his long body was collapsed in the chair. "You'd better tell us," he murmured at last, in an exhausted tone.

Nigel summarized the evidence. "You see, it *does* look bad for Mark," he ended.

"I *don't* believe it, Nigel," May said. "It would mean Mark was either a fiend or a madman. It must have been accidental."

"Yes, May, but you can't get round the article about carbon tetrachloride found in Chester's cupboard. Either he'd read it, and would be extremely careful about the use of cleaning fluid; or Mark had read it, and planted it there to give us the impression of suicide."

"In point of fact, they both knew," said the Master wearily.

"What? How?" Nigel's voice was sharp.

"It was at a party here, during the last semester. One or two of the Medical Faculty came along. There was a discussion about the possible toxic effects of cleaning fluids under certain conditions. Mark and Chester were both present. Don't you remember, May?"

"No. I wasn't there. Remember, it was a stag party?"

"To be sure. So it was."

"Did either of them show particular interest, Zeke? Ask questions?" Nigel asked.

"I guess not. It's not their line, after all. It's difficult to remember so far back. No, wait a minute. By God, I think Mark *did* say at some point it would be a cunning method if you wanted to murder someone. But it wouldn't have meant anything. I'm sure he was just aiming to turn the conversation into a lighter vein: all that technical detail became a bit tedious for us laymen."

May gazed anxiously at Nigel. "You mean, they'll arrest him any moment now?"

"Not quite. There's a lot of practical investigation to be done first. Looking for fingerprints on the magazine. Interviewing everyone who was at the party last night. Everything really hinges on that."

"The tray?" Zeke asked.

"Exactly. If they can get firm evidence that it was Chester who knocked the coffee over on himself, it's a point in Mark's favor."

"A point! It'd be decisive," said May stoutly.

"Would it? We all know Chester is accident-prone. And he was abnormally squiffed too. Mark might well have banked on his doing something clumsy," Zeke said.

"Och, you're the devil's advocate." His wife sighed.

"I doubt if the police will get any definite lead from the eye-witnesses. Did *you* see how the tray got tipped, Zeke?"

"No. I was talking to Charles Reilly when it happened."

After a pause, May said, "It'd come hard for Mark, whatever happens."

"How do you mean?"

"Mr. Ahlberg senior has a scunner of drink, since—but you know all about that. And he just needs an excuse to get his knife into poor Mark again. He'd work it up into a drunken brawl, with Mark throwing coffee at his brother. Disgraceful behavior in public again."

"Oh, come, May! Mark was sober enough."

"Well, then, the old ruffian will say he was sober enough to remember the dangers of carbon-whatever-it-is, and was criminally negligent to drench his brother with the stuff. The bathrooms are far too hot here anyway, Zeke. You should do something about it. The young men should be clean, not steamed alive like lobsters."

"I'll bear the point in mind, my dear," Zeke said dryly.

"Have you seen Mark today?" asked Nigel.

"No. He rang to beg off a Humanities tutors' meeting this morning. Said he was not feeling too grand."

"No wonder. He must have inhaled some of the fumes too."

"Did he know about his brother being taken to the Infirmary?" May asked.

"No," said Zeke. "I told him."

"How did he take it?"

"Shocked. Distressed. Naturally."

"His actual words—d'you remember them? This is important," Nigel said.

The Master was silent a moment, trying to recollect. "He said, 'Oh, not *again*.' Then, 'The Infirmary, did you say? But I thought he'd just passed out. Is he seriously ill? I must get along to see him.' "

"That all?"

"About Chester, yes. Perfectly natural, innocent words. Well, Nigel, surely you agree?"

"It's what he *didn't* say that worries me. Isn't it strange he didn't ask *what* was wrong with Chester? Suggests he already knew."

"Oh, really, Nigel, that's being too clever altogether. He'd just waked up. He was dazed."

"What puzzles me is the 'Oh, not *again*,' " May put in. "But it doesn't sound to my ear like the remark of a guilty man. More like a first spontaneous reaction: 'Oh, Lord, now we're in trouble again—we—Chester and I.' "

Nigel glanced at her with respect. The Master broke out, his bony head wagging in bewilderment, "It's getting more difficult every day to talk to those two naturally. First you tell me Chester is the chief suspect, then Mark. And I'm supposed to meet them as if none of this had happened."

"Don't meet them then," said Nigel heartlessly. "It won't go on much longer, anyway."

"I certainly hope not. Just now I feel as if it's a crime that will never be solved, and I'll have to go through with the rest of my Mastership knowing I have a murderer on my staff."

"Better than having a murder on your conscience," said May in her matter-of-fact way.

"I don't think that's a very helpful contribution, May." There was a vibration of anger beneath Zeke's level voice.

"Well," replied his wife comfortably, "*I* shall just go on treating Mark and Chester as I've always done. There's no use imagining bogles—wait till one jumps out at you."

A studious silence prevailed as Nigel strolled around in the great court. But for chinks of light showing beneath shades here and there, Hawthorne House might have been deserted—the scene of some terrene catastrophe, loitering through the night like an abandoned *Marie Celeste*. The town traffic could be heard distantly, a sea sussuration rising and falling. The stars were visible in their thousands; beyond them, invisible, millions more.

"A worm's-eye view," Nigel muttered. Everything here was so clean, so clear-cut and lucid: he felt a pang of nostalgia for muddled, smoky London. The clarity of New England was deceptive, though; not because it concealed dark mysteries, but because the sophisticated European projected his own subtleties and velleities upon it.

The American mind, Nigel thought, was not subtle. It could be extremely complex, but it worked efficiently by delimiting its activities: like a child setting out all its toys on the nursery floor and moving in due order from one to another. It seemed to him that an American had a built-in appointments book, which told him what he should be doing at every hour of the day: his constitution was a written one, as his private life was a mass of neatly interlocking schedules. There was not enough "play"—in the physicist's sense—in his microcosm. That probably explained, Nigel felt, what he'd decided was a nationwide recourse to psychoanalysts, and the outbreaks of violence by those who could not afford them. It was this rigidity of mind, this lack of "give," which drove men mad—an excess of mental orderliness spilling out into psychic disorder.

". . . while of unsound mind," he mused. It was not the passionate, unpremeditated act, though, which should be defined thus, but the long, warped course of action. "In dreams begin responsibilities"; and in fantasy begins a murderer's irresponsibility. The murderer here is a child, a clever child who never doubted he could make his fantasies come true; a pure egotist unable to take seriously the pitfalls through which he will pick his way, though his precocious intellect may plan carefully to avoid them.

And whom does all this point to?

Nigel went up to his room, with one last look at the night sky. He was undressing when the telephone rang.

"I've been trying to get you for ages—" the pure contralto

voice seemed to be throbbing right against his ear, as if she had put her lips to it. "Can you come and have lunch here tomorrow?"

"Yes, I'd like to. By the way, how are you?"

But Sukie rang off without another word.

13 ☞ "Danaë, in a Brazen Tower"

Three students joined Nigel at his table in the House dining hall. They set down their loaded breakfast trays and punctiliously shook hands with him.

"I hear Mr. Ahlberg is sick," said Philip.

"Yes."

"Nothing serious, I hope."

"Well, he's in the Infirmary, but—"

"Heaven help him then!" said Cyrus.

"Oh, hey," Philip protested. "They have a perfectly good staff of doctors there."

"*You* have to say so. The butcher's union. Philip is studying medicine."

"You understand Cyrus' field is medieval history, sir," said the pink-cheeked Philip. "That's where he gets *his* wide knowledge of medicine."

"There's a rumor he was poisoned somehow," said the third student, a beady-eyed young man with a crew cut. "Is that true, sir?"

"Some strange poison unknown to science," jeered Cyrus.

"Oh, no. It was just carbon tetrachloride," Nigel said.

"Good God, how did he get exposed to that?" Philip asked.

Nigel gave him an edited version of the cleaning-fluid episode.

"Gosh! I know a bit about that. I was given an assignment on that sort of stuff during the spring semester."

"Imagine the Faculty holding drunken parties! T'ck, t'ck. I have always suspected it," grinned Cyrus.

"Oh, lay off. The poor overworked guys, they have to unwind sometimes." The third student was smiling too.

"I'm glad you admit we're overworked," said Mark, putting his tray down on the table. "Mind if I join you?"

"Oh. Sorry. I'm sorry to hear about your brother," said Philip, blushing. He blushed readily, even at other people's *faux pas*.

Cyrus turned to the tutor. "Philip was just going to explain about carbon tetrachloride. He'd had a whole course on it or something."

"We experimented with rats, actually. There was a controlled experiment in the path lab."

"I don't want to hear much more about it," said Mark. "I'm still feeling a bit queasy myself."

"Not a hangover, I trust, Mr. Ahlberg?" inquired Cyrus solicitously.

"Thanks for the sympathy. But tutors do not get hangovers. I guess I inhaled a goodly amount of those fumes," said Mark.

"So what would your treatment be, my good doctor," asked Cyrus, "for carbon tetrachloride? He charges only a hundred dollars for an opinion, Mr. Ahlberg."

Philip blushed. "Well, I'd say a course of promethazine would protect against damage to the liver."

"What was that? I'd better lay in some, for next time I have to clean a suit. The stuff is dangerous," said Mark. "Can I buy it from any druggist, whatever it is, Philip?"

"Yes. In the form of Phenergan tablets."

"The blessings of science. Everything available," remarked Cyrus. "But what, we must ask ourselves, are the side effects of this lovely promethazine? Medical science is always chasing its own tail. It discovers a new disease: *then* it discovers a cure for it: *then* the cure sets up another disease. And so on ad infinitum. I suppose that's why doctors will never be out of work."

"Oh, sure! And if you'd had your way, I expect we'd still be squatting 'round alembics waiting for base metal to turn into gold, or counting the angels on the head of a pin."

Presently the students departed, still arguing vigorously.

When they'd gone Mark, who'd been staring into his coffee cup, looked up. "Why won't they let me visit Chester?"

"Won't they?"

"I rang up to inquire after him last night, and they said he was going along all right but no visitors were allowed. They have no right to forbid his own family to see him."

"They have to keep him under observation, I dare say."

A forlorn, rather childish expression came over Mark's face. "You're not holding out on me? Is Brady behind this?"

"Is that what's worrying you?"

"I'm worrying about Chester." Mark's glance was opaque. "But I'd not put it past Brady to think I'd done it deliberately."

"What—the cleaning fluid? *You* couldn't know it might have a toxic effect. Could you?"

"That's the hell of it. I *could* have." Mark's voice became confidential. "There was some talk about it once at one of Zeke's parties. I didn't take it all that seriously then. Wish I had. But, after all, millions of people use the stuff every day."

"Well, *Chester* seems to have been reading up on it." Nigel told him about the journal found in the cupboard.

"Oh, Chester. He's always fussing about health. Always taking precautions."

"How *did* it all happen, in fact? The stuff getting spilled and what followed."

Mark's face darkened. "Always on the job, aren't you?"

"Well, not always. But just show me. Exactly."

Mark sighed, took up one of the breakfast trays, and moved to Nigel's side. "You're Chester, on the sofa. I stand in front of you. Just as I'm about to take hold of the coffee pot, you half rise and bump into the tray. The movement knocks the pot forward toward you, and upsets the milk saucepan too. The lid of the pot falls, and you get coffee and milk over you, before the pot rolls off onto the carpet. Happy? Or shall we try a physical reconstruction?"

"No. That's enough," replied Nigel abstractedly.

"It was just one of those damned unfortunate little accidents. Neither of us was overly sober. Chester was certainly loaded enough to—not to realize he'd bumped his hand against the tray, and to think I'd done the damage. It's all so trivial. Surely *somebody* must have seen what happened?"

"Those two friends of his were nearest, but they had their backs to the sofa."

"I gather the idea is that *I* organized the accident so as to have a good excuse for rubbing down poor old Chester with that damned fluid and—? For Chrissake! Do you really think, if I wanted to kill anyone, I'd use such a haphazard method?" Mark was becoming highly indignant, though he kept his voice down to avoid being noticed by students at nearby tables.

"Sorry to nag about this, but you said Chester bumped his *hand* against the tray. Did you actually see this happen?"

Mark paused for thought. "No. It was all too fast, and I wasn't paying attention. I have a sort of impression of his hand near the tray and the coffee pot falling over."

There was a silence, in which the voice of an undergraduate two tables away could be heard clearly enunciating, "What is your opinion on the Milton controversy, Mr. Reilly?"

"Not at breakfast, me boy. Anyway, Milton's unreadable. What's the use of God in the head if you've only sawdust in the belly?"

Mark, distracted for a moment, rolled up his eyes at Nigel. "Oh, that Charles. I suppose that's the British method—stimulating the pupil to think, by shoveling emetic views down his throat." Then coming back to his own problem, he lowered his voice. "You know this place is a hotbed of rumor: it's only a matter of time before my father hears some gossip about me poisoning Chester; and then—"

"Then you've had it? Well, now, Mark, I don't know. But would you mind so much, being cut out of his will?"

"To tell you the truth, Nigel, I couldn't care less. So long as it didn't mean my being drummed out of university teaching." . . .

Sukie Tate opened the door for Nigel. The day was overcast, and in her shabby apartment she looked frail and pale, peeping out of the fog. There was an unwontedly subdued expression on her face, with its dark smudges under her eyes.

"How are you, Sukie?"

"I'm so glad you came. Somehow I never thought you would," she said shyly, lowering her long lashes.

"Why ever not?"

"Well, last time seems so long ago. And there was prison in between." She bit her lip. "A few days in prison are like years. You got further and further away. A stranger."

"I would have come to see you there. Why wouldn't you let me?"

Her beautiful eyes swept slowly up to his. "Because, because. Sit down and I'll pour you a drink. No, not that end of the sofa—there's a spring broken. Would you like some bourbon?—water? —soda?"

"Soda would be nice. Did they treat you all right?"

"They didn't beat me up or anything. It's the loneliness. Here you are. I won't have to go back, will I?" she asked in a childish tone of appeal.

"I hope not."

"It was kind of Master Edwardes to spring me. He's a good man, isn't he?"

"Yes. Has your father been here?"

"I don't want to talk about him, Nigel. I guess I haven't been fair to him. But he's finished, down and out: just a shadow of— of what he used to be."

"And John?"

"Oh, Nigel, I'm terribly, terribly anxious about him. They let me see him before I left. It was a dreadful shock. He seems to have given up. Like Dad. I was afraid it would happen."

"Which was why you made that absurd confession."

"I—yes, I thought it would take the heat off him for a little. Oh, I don't know *what* I thought. It's such a waste. He's so brilliant. And now I don't know if—if he can ever—sort of rehabilitate himself."

"Zeke will take him back. I'm sure of that."

Her gray eyes opened wide. "Oh, do you really mean that? He will? Wouldn't it be wonderful!"

"And, Sukie, the first stage of rehabilitation will be for you to snip the apron strings. I mean it. Now, don't glare at me, dear child! John must learn to stand on his own feet, emotionally and morally. So cut out the little-mother act. You're too bossy by half."

"Well, I *must* say!"

" 'Love is proved in the letting go'—that's what an English poet wrote." Nigel got up and moved to the desk by the window. "I see *you*'ve got yourself working again." He pointed at the books and papers lying on it.

"Oh, yes. That Emily. Yes, I've been trying to get back to her. It isn't easy, and I'm afraid I'll have to change my supervisor."

"Mark? Why on earth—?"

"You see I'm writing to tell him I can't marry him. It wouldn't work. It just wouldn't," she said bleakly. "No, we'll talk about it over lunch. I must go and dish it up. You make yourself comfortable."

Nigel prowled about the room. It was a student's room, untidy, rather impersonal, giving the impression that Sukie bivouacked here only, and tomorrow would be on the march again. Her few belongings moved him strangely: a row of graduated elephants among the invitations on the mantel, a box crusted with seashells, a pair of green suede shoes.

"Now tell me why you're not going to marry Mark," he said as they sat down to a risotto and salad.

"I don't want to get him into any more trouble. His lousy father would—"

"Being quixotic again? Now the real reason."

Sukie looked straight into his eyes. "I don't love him. Not enough."

"Well, you know best. But I wouldn't mail your letter yet. Mark is in bad enough trouble without that. But maybe you didn't know?"

"No. I don't know. What's happened?"

Nigel told her.

"Oh, damn! That alters everything. I must—"

"No, you mustn't. Stick to him because he's in a jam, I mean. Pity is no substitute for love, and you should know it," he said.

"Now *you're* being bossy."

"I'd like some more of this delicious risotto."

"Okay." She smiled demurely, taking his plate. "You *do* eat fast." Her breast brushed his shoulder as she returned.

He ate for a few minutes, then said, "By the way, Charles told me you broke it off with Chester because he frightened you. Is that so?"

"Oh, Charles! It wasn't *that* serious. It was just—Chester dated me some—"

"How did he frighten you?" Nigel persisted.

The girl pondered. "Nothing he did, or said. He's always polite. You see he intrigued me. I felt he was different from other tutors —from most men I met. I thought he had great potential drive, if only—"

"If only a good woman brought it out." Nigel smiled at her.

"Now you're laughing at me. There was something—oh, hell—self-contained about him that attracted me."

"The well-known box had the same effect on Pandora."

"And something remote too. He had no real friends either." Sukie knitted her brows. "You know, latterly I got to feel he was —well, like an ordinary automobile with a souped-up engine, and if I tried to drive it, it would get out of my control and there'd be an accident. I mean, there were times I was with him when I felt I just wasn't there, for him. And I"—she averted her face —"didn't like the way he tried to make love; as if I was some kind of mechanical doll and he was reading from a book of instructions. He was difficult to be alone with."

"Did he never introduce you to his friends, colleagues?"

"Well, not often, I guess. There were two on the Business Faculty. We saw them once or twice. A man called Andreyevsky and—"

"Yes, I met him at the party. And Chester wasn't too upset, didn't make a scene when you broke it off?"

" 'Break off' is too dramatic. I just sort of discontinued with him. Anyhow he'd be too proud, in his funny little way, to make scenes."

"And then Mark came along?" he asked.

"Oh, the three of us had been going around together quite a time before that. After Chester and I drifted apart, Mark didn't steal me from him: Mark's *much* too honorable for that. But when he became my supervisor, naturally we had to see a lot of each other. And I was at a loose end. And he's fun to be with."

"But no drive?"

Sukie glanced at Nigel suspiciously. "Well, I dunno. He does such crazy things. Breaks out—you know? Times, it made me uncomfortable. Like a sort of act. As if it all came off the top of his head."

"And what goes on underneath?"

"How should I know? You know, I guess I don't understand much about men. I never imagined Charles Reilly would be like that, for instance. But Mark— You know that zany smile of his; and the way he suddenly yells with laughter. You feel it's really some joke he's sharing with nobody but himself. Sometimes I've wondered does he care for *anything* much except English literature. But he does make some very fine discriminations there—I'll give him that."

Nigel suppressed a smile. "And when *he* made love to you?"

She looked at him strangely. "You do ask a lot of questions. Will you have some dessert?"

"An apple, please."

Sukie fetched a dish from a side table. "They're Canadian."

"Are they? Splendid. They look like wax fruit. Too red to be true."

She polished one on her sleeve and handed it to him. "Does Clare cook for you?"

He smiled quickly. "Why, yes. Extremely well. But you were going to tell me about Mark."

Sukie pouted at him. "Was I? Oh, well, if I must. Let's see. He was tender, and considerate, I guess. But he always makes— made me feel as if he had something else on his mind. As if he ought to prove something to himself, as if I was a sort of test he had to pass and couldn't quite bring himself to go through with in case he failed. He'll *say* anything: but, you know, I think he's very repressed underneath—he won't let himself go. Not with women. Not with me, at any rate."

"So you never went to bed together?"

She blushed, turning her head away. "No."

"Perhaps *you* made *him* shy."

She looked toward him. "Do I make you feel shy?"

"That's another matter."

A constraint had risen between them. She broke it by leaning forward, taking his hand; then she led him to the sofa and curled up on the floor beside him, her arms stretched across his knees.

"When are you going back to Britain?" she asked.

"Next week, I think."

There was another silence.

"I wouldn't—I don't want to take you away from Clare. I know I couldn't," she whispered—and then something he was unable to catch.

"What did you say, Sukie?"

She lifted her head, gazed with a sort of tremulous resolution into his eyes. "Just once. I thought about you all the time in prison. Don't you want me?"

"Susannah dear, are you trying to turn me into one of the Elders?"

"No. No. *They* only looked. I don't like *voyeurs*. And I'm tired of men who only want their mothers."

"Like John?" he asked.

"And Mark. Aren't I beautiful enough for you?"

"You're a lovely girl, Sukie."

She arched her back, and her breasts pushed up at him. "Nigel. Darling. Make me forget everything—everything but you. Just once."

Then she was in his lap. Oh, well, he sighed to himself. Her kisses were swarming all over him. Wherever they touched, delicious messages fluttered between them.

"Undress me," she cried blindly. Then, "No, wait, I'll call you."

When she called, he went into the bedroom. She was naked on the narrow bed, breathing fast, her hair tumbled over the pillow, her exquisite small body shivering with impatience.

Soon, her nails raked down his back and she was giving sharp cries—louder and louder till it seemed as if the little room would explode. She tossed her arms above her head; the hands clenched into fists, then slowly uncurled as the last cry died away and the arms were stretched out limp on either side. Her body slackened, caved in, seemed to dissolve beneath him.

"Oh glory," she sighed. "Oh glory oh glory."

They drowsed for a while. Then she raised her head from his shoulder. "What do you like best about me?"

He considered the question gravely. "That you've never used the dreary phrase 'having sex.' And I like your not fawning on me after I'd made love to you. Or becoming obviously triumphant, or complacent, or possessive."

"Like most women?"

"Like some women."

Another silence. She traced the cage of his ribs with a finger like a feather. "Now, what are you thinking?"

"I was wondering if you *really* knew about John and Josiah Ahlberg—which of them pinched the other's ideas?"

"Oh, Nigel, *must* you? I honestly don't know. I *think* it must have been Josiah, because I don't believe John would dare to make an accusation like that unless he'd got really mad with Josiah—been driven to it—so he could ignore the consequences. I mean for a student to challenge— But I've no proof." She leaned over him, her gray eyes questioning his suspiciously. "You *didn't* plan all this to wring a confession out of me, off my guard?"

"No, dear Sukie. No. I assure you of that."

She flung back the sheet, and her hand strolled about on him. "*I* was wondering something, too."

"Yes?"

"Whether you'd care to have sex with me again."

"Now you've really asked for trouble!" exclaimed Nigel.

"Give it to me then." . . .

The lamps had lit up on the paths across the Common when Nigel walked back, in a daze but without regrets. Surely there were none for Sukie either. Kissing him good-by, she had been lustrous and innocent as a Christmas tree; had asked him if he would stay with her for his last days in Cabot. "I'd love to," he had said. "But we might become an addiction for each other. And that would never do." And she accepted it, shining at him. "It's all right, Nigel my darling. It's fine. I shall be all right now. Don't worry about me. I feel like—like Danaë. After the shower of gold. Oh, that's not fawning, is it?"

He'd touched her check gently and they'd said they would never forget each other; and they never would.

Nigel continued to walk slowly until he got to K entrance in Emerson House, where he studied the name board, saw *Mr. S. Andreyevsky,* and climbed one flight of stairs. He had arranged the interview by telephone from Sukie's flat, much to her interest. Andreyevsky opened the door and welcomed him hospitably: a solemn, unsmiling young man, he was too polite to ask at once the reason for Nigel's visit. First he inquired after "the health of my esteemed colleague, Chester Ahlberg," was assiduous with drinks and cigarettes, spoke about Cabot's chances in the Yale game on Saturday and his admiration for London.

"Do you come over to London often, Mr. Andreyevsky?" Nigel asked.

"Alas, not as often as I could wish. I haven't visited Britain but the once a year ago—nearly fifteen months in fact. But it is all very vivid to me, and it will be so."

Nigel found it curiously difficult to get past the barrage of words and approach his objective. Somehow he felt that to make his bizarre request would be like asking a floorwalker at Fortnum & Mason's what color were his underpants.

"You know the Ahlbergs pretty well, I suppose," he temporized.

"Well, you can say that in respect of Chester certainly. We went through college together, and found each other highly congenial. Of course we had met first at our preparatory school, St. Paul's, but I actually didn't see so much of him there. He was in a different set. Though I do remember we were assigned the parts of Sebastian and Viola in one end-of-term production—in the comedy *Twelfth Night*, by Shakespeare."

"And Mark Ahlberg?" Nigel cut down on the reminiscences.

"Well, I got acquainted with *him* through his brother, after I obtained my tutorship at Cabot."

"A nice fellow."

Andreyevsky considered the proposition. "Well, yes. That is to say, he's a very popular tutor, from what I hear."

"But you have reservations?"

"Well, frankly, in conversation with him, I've found his stance toward my own area of study a little—how shall I phrase it?—a little frivolous. With a father like his, I'd have figured he'd appreciate more keenly than he does the paramount importance today of all that comes within the ambit of commercial and industrial relations."

"All this fiddle with literature?" Nigel asked.

"I don't mean that, exactly. I have great respect for the achievement of those who are eminent in the cultural field. It's in the context of broader contemporary issues that I find Mark's viewpoint somewhat circumscribed."

"I see your point."

"Apart from which," Andreyevsky ground on, "he's not overly reliable. Chester has found him somewhat of an embarrassment on occasion. It's a certain lack of maturity, of a responsible attitude."

"Not a good citizen?"

"I think you've put your finger on it, Mr. Strangeways." The host nodded with portentous approval. "But I hope these most unfortunate occurrences in Hawthorne House may compel Mark to, er—"

"To grow up?"

"Precisely."

Nigel took a swig of his bourbon. "You may have heard," he said, adapting his pace to Andreyevsky's funereal one, "that I am acting for Master Edwardes in an advisory capacity over these unfortunate occurrences."

"So Chester has told me."

"It's on this subject that I wished to see you tonight."

"Ah, yes. I see. But I don't exactly see how *I* could be of any assistance to you there."

Nigel could not keep up the slow march any longer. "What I want is to see your passport."

"My *passport?*" Andreyevsky took off his horn-rimmed spectacles, as if to get a better view of this extraordinary request.

"Yes. If you'll be so kind."

"But that's—I mean—how can it possibly—?" The tutor's measured periods had broken up like a log jam.

"I am not at liberty to divulge the reason for this request," said Nigel impressively. "I can only assure you of its relevance."

"Why, certainly, then. *I've* certainly no objection." He began to root around in the paper-stuffed drawers of a bureau. "I guess it's somewhere here. As I mentioned, I haven't had occasion to use it for quite a time. Ah, here we are."

He handed the passport to Nigel. Who held his breath as he flipped over the pages. "Look there," he said.

"But I said I'd visited Britain."

"Yes. But it has *two* date stamps."

"But that's impossible. I've traveled there only once." Andreyevsky put on his spectacles again, to scrutinize the document more closely—or prevent his eyes falling out with astonishment. "Yes. Why, that's only three weeks ago. I don't understand it. I really don't."

"Nobody, to your knowledge, has borrowed it?"

"Borrowed it! Certainly not. You know passports aren't transferable."

"Have you missed it from the drawer any time during the last month?"

"No. Mind you, it's a drawer I use only for documents I seldom need to refer to. Such as my will, for example. And certain testimonials. Birth certificate. That sort of thing."

"I suppose some of your friends would know you kept the passport there?"

"My friends? Possibly. I couldn't say for certain, but it *could* be possible."

"Do you remember any of them asking to see it?"

The tutor thought hard. "I can't say that I do. There have been—no, no, I'm *wrong*. I remember Chester and Mark and some other people were here one night—in April, I seem to remember. And we got talking about passport photographs. Mark asked me to show him mine. They're always so startling. They razzed me about it a bit. But that was all."

"Was Chester interested?"

"Not particularly, I'd say."

Nigel rose. "Well, I'm grateful to you. Got a key to the drawer?"

"Why, yes, I do. But I don't always remember to lock it."

"Well, put the passport back, and lock the drawer, and don't let go of the key."

Andreyevsky did as he was asked. "I would be interested to know why you're interested. Would you want to tell me what this is all about?"

"You've got state exhibit Number One in there."

"Is that so?" His face was lively with interest, and his language had come down off its perch now that his curiosity had been aroused. "What you're saying—somebody took my passport and *used* it? But how would that be possible? It would have to be someone who looked just like me—or faked the photo to look like him."

"Or faked himself to look like the photo. And not much faking needed."

"But what in the world did he want to do that for? Didn't he possess a passport of his own? He must have been in a hell of a hurry to get somewhere if he couldn't apply for one."

"He was certainly in a hurry."

"But who?" asked Andreyevsky.

"Can't say now. I will know soon enough. Have to go." And Nigel left.

Back at Hawthorne, Nigel phoned Lieutenant Brady, only to be told he was out of town for the night—maybe two.

"Did he leave any message for me?"

"Yep. Said to tell you he's following a new lead; figured it'd give him a piece of clinching evidence to complete the case."

"Case against whom?"

"Mark Ahlberg. Who else?"

Nigel put paper and carbon into his typewriter, removed his

jacket, and set to work. He had not finished the first page before his head nodded and he fell asleep. He was wakened by loud knocking on the door. Charles Reilly stood outside. Brushing past Nigel, he gave the typewriter a casual glance and plunked himseld down in the best armchair.

"I didn't know you were a writer."

"I'm composing a letter," Nigel explained.

"Where've you been all day? I tried to get you."

"I've been bored to extinction, and run to earth a great treasure in the process. Before that, I was seduced."

"D'you tell me so? Well, let's hope it'll make a better man of you. Y'know, I've sometimes wondered if you were human at all."

"What do you want, Charles?"

"A drink, for one thing."

"You can have one drink, and then I'm going to bed."

"Listen to him! Isn't bed where you've just come from? Sure, you've neither decency nor stamina. Tell me, lad, who's the enchantress?"

"Mind your own business, you prurient old pest! Here you are. Drink it up. Now, what *is* it you want?"

"Just to tell you I rang poor old Chester this afternoon and had a pleasant gab. He's much better, I'm glad to say. They'll discharge him in a day or two. Fit as anything. Why, when I told him I was taking you to the Yale game on Saturday, blessed if he didn't say *he'd* be there. Sure, him and football seem a queer combination, but he's got a ticket, he says, though it's nowhere near where we're sitting."

"And you woke me up to tell me *this?*" asked Nigel, outraged.

"Ah, well, will you wait now? I'm coming to the gravamen of my subject. Chester said also that he wanted to see his brother, or at least talk to him. So off I went and tried to find Mark, and I couldn't at all. Fella was last seen at a midday seminar. Seems he's canceled a lecture and some other engagements—didn't tell the Master he was going. And Zeke's worried about it."

"They're thinning out," Nigel muttered.

"But how did he manage to disappear like this? Sure, I thought the police were keeping an eye on him."

"So did I."

14 ☞ By Hand

What with one thing and another, Nigel was not able to complete his letter till the Friday evening, when a telephone call and conversation he'd had that day required additions. He took out the last page and the carbon copy from his typewriter, and laid them on the two heaps. He picked up the top copy and began to read:

Dear Ahlberg. The time has come to acquaint you with certain facts. Most of them you know, of course: some you may have suspected: but there are others which will give you an unpleasant shock.

The murder of Josiah Ahlberg, the practical jokes and the episode of the cleaning fluid (which might be described as the culminating or pay-off joke) were all part of a pattern and the work of one man. The man is you.

What were your motives? Hostility to Josiah, for one of several possible reasons: greed (or need) for money: fear of some exposure.

The more I thought about the original crime and its subsidiaries the more they convinced me as the work of a person who was (a) extremely clever, (b) extraordinarily naïve, (c) fantastically lucky. They were like a mimic campaign, brilliantly planned on paper by an academic staff; the umpires would see men falling, but these would get up and go home at the day's end, and the planners were concerned only with maps, timetables and logistics.

In plain words, you have no sense of reality. In plainer words still, you are mad.

But it is a calculating madness. You planned, as an abstract thing, not only your offensive but your lines of retreat. And it was your madness upon which you could in the last resort fall back.

You are also an academic; and this led you to overcomplicating things. You arranged that not only your brother but John Tate should come under suspicion, for example. And this was your downfall.

You were given the "news" of Josiah's death, you got very angry because you "hadn't been told sooner." You *knew* that Josiah had been shot on the Thursday night, yet it was not till five days later that you were informed of the murder. You could not know John Tate would conceal the body. And why would you assume there'd been a five-day delay in telling you about the murder, unless you'd committed it yourself?

I only discovered this disastrous reaction of yours when I talked with Mark today, who'd been away secretly visiting your father, to tell him the facts about the carbon tetrachloride episode before a more sinister interpretation of it came to his ears.

I am not a censorious man, but I have nothing but contempt for the way, time and again, and with repellent subtlety, you tried to poison our minds against Mark—sugar-coated poison pills. I don't think you hated him, except perhaps when Sukie left you for him: little megalomaniacs feel superior to hatred. Mark was just in your way, as Josiah was. You coveted the *whole* of your father's estate (had you plans for knocking him off later or were you in a "we-can-wait" frame of mind so far as he was concerned?).

You were so insensately ambitious, and so humorless, with your absurd paper plans for what you would do with all that money and power. You conveyed it to me—do you remember?—on that trip to Concord, when you also conveyed something a great deal more fatal to your scheme.

I used the phrase "the mourners shuttling back and forth." It made you come over queer, for it associated in your mind with the New York shuttle plane; and this enabled me to see how your alibi could be broken.

Of course, only a megalomaniac would—not have the fantastic

luck—but envisage what luck would be needed to pull off such a scheme. You know the details—how you flew back here via New York shortly after you'd arrived in London, shot your brother, and returned in time for your first conference in London. Did you ever think about the multiplicity of things, all along the line, which might have gone wrong? I doubt it. Your crazy self-confidence (which you very effectively concealed) would have surmounted such trivial details.

But you had to use Andreyevsky's passport for the secret journey. A false mustache was all you needed—hadn't you and he played Sebastian and Viola once? But the passport is stamped by the British authorities for the day you returned to London; and that cooks your goose: as well as the fact that an Andreyevsky is down on the passenger lists, Lieutenant Brady has just told me, of two separate airlines, one flying to New York on that Thursday morning and the other returning at midnight.

The revolver, I've little doubt, was thrown off a bridge into the Thames. It's significant that, with all the resources of the police over here, it should never have been found.

The night you shot Josiah you'd faked a note from him to Mark, so you had one "suspect" on the scene of the crime shortly afterward. And I don't believe you ever arranged an interview between Josiah and John Tate—your brother wouldn't have consented: you just *told* Sukie you'd arranged it. So there was another "suspect" in position.

But what would you have done if Josiah hadn't been working in his office, as he usually did? Gone to his house and killed him? Called the operation off? We shall never know. Until you confess. Being the person you are, you'd never commit yourself to a crime before you actually committed it: you would always leave yourself a loophole.

Which brings me to the practical jokes. They were intended to work two ways. If they were pinned on Mark, it would create a scandal which might well get him cut out of your father's will. But if the worst came to the worst, and you were arraigned for murder, you would confess to having done them yourself. Think what a powerful plea your advocate could make! Only a deranged mind could play nasty jokes on its owner. The prisoner therefore is off his head, not fit to stand trial—or at least not to be sent to the electric chair.

What interests me most, though, is the light these jokes shed upon your character. That placard outside the hall made a fool of you. Only a monomaniac could face the idea of turning himself publicly into a figure of fun. But you didn't mind—though you put up a great show of indignation: you were above such petty contumelies, hugging to yourself your cherished objective, your secret knowledge of the power you had and the vaster power you aimed at.

This is indeed laughable, when one thinks how negligible you really are, what a total nonentity.

However, as the days went on, and Mark was not arrested, you had to give things a nudge. You brought a reserve plan into action. You had read about the effects of carbon tetrachloride. So you held that party, arranging favorable conditions for its operation. You appeared to drink far more than usual, neatly suggested to Mark that black coffee was needed, neatly spilled it over yourself in such a way that no one could be sure it wasn't he who'd done the spilling, and allowed yourself to be copiously rubbed down with the cleaning fluid.

The idea was to demonstrate that Mark had made a diabolical attempt on your life. Again, you were taking a chance: you could not be certain of steering events just the way you wanted them to go. But you relied on your brother's good nature, and it did not fail you.

What a fearful risk you were taking with your own life, though! Or were you? You certainly had a desperate look on your neat little face during the party. But, as usual, you had organized an out for yourself. You had discovered that promethazine, in the form of Phenergan tablets, counters the toxicity of carbon tetrachloride. You took some of the tablets before the party, so you were in no real danger. What you should have done was to hide the bottle of tablets better, not just leave them tucked at the back in your well-stocked medicine cupboard for me to find.

Apart from this blinding mistake, it was quite a clever attempt to get Mark in trouble again. This time you had the sense not to plant the evidence (the medical journal) in his room, as you did the copy of *Playboy,* but put them in your cupboard suggesting *he* had planted them on you.

And you weren't far from succeeding—it must be very riling for you. Brady favored your brother as the murderer; he might even have arrested him.

Do you know what May Edwardes calls you?—"the Organization Man." It's interesting how almost everyone I met here treated you, talked about you, in a kind of humoring, forbearing, allowance-making manner, ranging from mild contempt to compunction: only Mark seemed genuinely solicitous for you, at times. For him, blood was thicker than water. But you're so enclosed in your delusions of grandeur that you hardly noticed his affection for you, his protectiveness. He's just someone who was in your way. How could you understand human feeling when you're subhuman yourself?

But you did show one glimmer of it. When you heard that John Tate had been arrested, and later that his sister had "confessed," you became quite indignant. But alas, this was not a disinterested emotion. It was petulant fury at your plan going awry: for it was not they you wanted put away, but Mark, the man who stood between you and the whole of your father's fortune.

So there we have it—a mean plot and a mean murderer. Your madman's luck has run out at last.

What do you propose to do about it? You could shoot yourself, but you improvidently chucked the gun into the Thames. You could confess the whole thing to Brady. Or you could have another of your "nervous breakdowns." I don't know what to advise.

You have not much time to decide. Lieutenant Brady will get a copy of this letter tomorrow morning. If he has not already ordered your arrest, he will do so then: even your father's influence cannot stop it.

Yours etc. Nigel Strangeways

Nigel put the letter in an envelope, and walked round to the

Cabot Infirmary. There he was told that Chester Ahlberg was recovered; but since some final tests confirming this had only been made in the afternoon, he would not be discharged till tomorrow morning. He asked permission to deliver a letter by hand, and was directed to the second floor.

In the orderly's little room, its door open to give a full view of Chester's door, a plainclothes cop sat yawning. Nigel asked him when his relief would turn up. "Nine P.M. Coupla hours."

"I've a letter here for Mr. Ahlberg. Will you hand it to him right away?"

"Okay."

"You'll be returning to the station house before you go off duty?"

"Sure."

"Then will you please leave this one for Lieutenant Brady? He *must* see it the moment he gets in." Nigel handed the duplicate letter, with "Urgent" typed on the envelope.

"Why not give it to this Ahlberg yourself, mister?" asked the policeman, holding up the other letter. "You're free to go in."

"He'd keep me chatting. I'm in a hurry."

"Okay. Your word's my law," said the man sardonically.

"And there's this. Impress it on your relief that, if he doesn't get a message from the Lieutenant before Mr. Ahlberg leaves tomorrow morning, he must shadow him. He's got to stick on Ahlberg's tail as tight as a tick. It's top priority."

"Say, what's this? I figured we were here to protect the guy."

"You're here to see no more harm's done."

"You mean, somebody might try to bump him when he goes out of this morgue?"

"What—in a law-abiding city like this, officer?"

The man grinned at him.

"*Wherever* he goes, he must be followed. Like—" Nigel drew upon the vernacular—"like a wolf follows a well-stacked dame."

"Right. I get you."

It was a nuisance, though quite proper, thought Nigel as he walked back to Hawthorne, that Brady should have gone in person to New York to see the passenger lists and talk to witnesses; to say nothing of the sticky interview with Mr. Ahlberg senior. Of course, it would have been better to keep Chester under surveillance at the Infirmary till every detail of the case against him was sewed up: but this could only have been done by Brady's taking the hospital authorities into his confidence, which he was unwilling to do at this stage.

When Nigel left the hospital he went to see Mark Ahlberg. "Mark," he said abruptly as he came in, "what are you doing tomorrow?"

"Tomorrow? Why? Well, I've two pupils in the morning. Then there's the ball game."

"You're going to miss them all, I'm afraid," Nigel said. "You're going away for the weekend, starting early—*very early*."

"Nigel! Have you gone crazy?"

"I hear your brother's being discharged in the morning. I'm not taking any more risks."

Mark's look of bewilderment soon changed to one of intelligence and sadness. "Oh, I see. I was afraid of it, you know. Nigel, are you *absolutely* sure you're right?"

Nigel nodded.

"Oh, God! Poor old Chester."

15 ☞ Go Go Go!

For hours that night Chester Ahlberg
had felt his brain slowly, by infinitesimal degrees, dwindling and
hardening: it was now a small, sharp point. When he had first
read the letter, he had cowered physically under the impact of
Nigel's withering contempt. Then he tore it up—tore each page
into smaller and smaller fragments, as if to destroy it would cause
the past, and all that the letter said, to be nullified. But it couldn't
be, and the dispersed fragments of the past came together again,
and would not be evaded.

Or could be evaded only, with a tremendous mental wrench,
by a change of direction. It was Nigel Strangeways—the man
who had led him on and betrayed him—not Mark now, against
whom the small, sharp point was turned. "Mad," "humorless,"
"insensately ambitious," "negligible," "nonentity"—such words,
which had rankled so horribly, began to harden the purpose
within him. "I *can* hate. Whatever you say. I *can*," he muttered:
"you'll be sorry that you dared address me like that."

I am not crazy, he thought; but I can act madness, like Ham-
let. Bare bodkin. Act madness so they'll never send me to the
chair.

His mind kept repeating certain phrases, like a phonograph
record with a faulty groove. I am sane I am sane I am sane I am
sane. He pushed the needle on. I'll teach him I'll teach him I'll
teach him. Josiah's face blazed up suddenly huge in his mind, as

it had showed that Thursday night. "What on earth are you doing here? I thought you were supposed to be in Britain." Same tone of voice, ordering me about, questioning my every move, as if I was a boy still. Prig bully pedantic son of a bitch!

It is not enough to have power: one must be seen to have it, acknowledged as a man of power. The finger on the trigger has absolute power, but it is secret: an explosion, a timeless instant like an orgasm which takes away life instead of giving it; but this is an act of darkness. To kill in broad daylight, in the presence of thousands—that would be the greatest, the pinnacle of climax. . . .

Out of the hospital and seemingly healthy, seemingly sane, sitting in his warm room, Chester fondled his gigantic, audacious purpose. Its where and when had flashed on him during the night watches: its how lay on the desk before him—a stiletto brought back three years ago from Italy as a souvenir. Would he have time, though? He had left the Infirmary early, saying grateful good-bys to matron, nurses, registrar. No one had prevented his return to Hawthorne House. At 9:30 he had called Mark on the telephone: there was no reply. He assumed the plainclothes man detailed to protect him at the Infirmary would any minute now be warned by Brady to keep him cornered till reinforcements arrived. The man was outside his door, no doubt, or hanging about in the entrance.

Chester kept his ear cocked for the wail of a police-car siren. It all depended now upon timing and luck. Well, he'd been told he was fantastically lucky; but that was a sneer, a jealous refusal to admit the formidable power of achievement of his brain. He felt wonderfully brisk and bright and cold, like the weather outside his window: a fine day for the game.

Another hour passed. What *were* they waiting for? Chester began to feel disquieted. How much longer would he have to wait, dressed up in his black overcoat and black kid gloves, the fedora on the desk beside him? Was it some trick they were playing, some way of breaking his nerve? Or perhaps Brady had not yet received Strangeways' letter. Stupid bastards, standing him up like this! Chester allowed that other self within him to master and dictate to him—surrendered to it, as a woman to a lover, or an athlete to his trainer.

A little before midday he heard the police-car siren. He rose, put on his hat, slid the stiletto up his left sleeve, opened the door gently. No one outside. The lock clicked behind him. His rubber-soled shoes were silent on the stone stairway. He peered downward at its first turning. A broad back stood in the entrance, looking left to the main gateway. Chester drew the stiletto from his left sleeve. He could not see the police reinforcements, but they must be moving across the court now, for the plainclothes man hailed them—moved down the steps outside the entrance to meet them. And, as he did so, Chester moved silently down the stairs, turned right, and continued on, down another flight into the basement passages.

He could hear, behind him, a voice saying, "Hi, fellas! He's still up there. Hasn't been a peep outa him."

Chester strode along the underground passages, the stiletto in his pocket now.

"Nice to see you back, Mr. Ahlberg," said a student coming the other way. "I hear you've been sick. I hope you're feeling better."

"Thanks, Pete. I feel fine."

Chester climbed stairs again, up to one of the House's side entrances, took a bicycle from a stand outside, and pedaled off leisurely. Apart from that one student, he had not encountered anyone. Who in hell said his luck had run out? . . .

Sukie Tate was sitting at her desk by the window. Sheets of

paper, covered with her sprawling handwriting, lay in front of her. She'd got the thesis running again, after a day or two during which Nigel had ousted Emily Dickinson from her mind. She felt serenely happy, not a twinge of regret, or of annoyance that Nigel had not returned to her after that first visitation. For so it seemed to her now—a visitation, a lovely, unearned, unexpected bonus. Not that you didn't work for it, my girl, she thought, smiling secretively: but now you must get on with real life.

Nevertheless, when her doorbell rang, she leapt up eagerly. Perhaps Nigel had changed his mind.

"Why, *Chester!*" she exclaimed. Even he, in his present state of mind, noticed how her face fell.

"You were expecting Mark?" he asked hopefully.

"Oh, no," she said in some confusion. "I— Come right in, Chester. You startled me. I didn't know they'd let you out of hospital."

"Yes, I'm fine now. Thought I'd drop in."

"It's nice to see you," Sukie said, a little nervously. "May I take your coat?"

"That's all right. I know where to hang it."

He hung up his coat in the hall closet. There was another man's coat there, an old tweed one. A brilliant improvisation came to him. "Sukie, is that coat John's? Could I borrow it for the afternoon? I'm going to the Yale game, and mine's rather thin for this cold weather."

"Sure you may," she called out.

"Thanks a lot."

"Now, will you have a drink?"

Chester transferred the stiletto to one pocket of the tweed coat, and to the other a woolen balaclava helmet he extracted from an inside pocket of his black overcoat.

"Cheers," he said, raising the glass. "You look different, Sukie."

The lineaments of gratified desire, she thought, smiling like a cat. "So do you, Chester."

He gave her a suspicious glance. "I've been sick. Remember?"

"Should you go to the game?"

"It'll do me good. Fresh air. You wouldn't have a bite for me to eat, would you?"

"Why, of course, Chester." Odder and odder, she thought. "I'll fix something. Make yourself comfortable."

He relaxed in this chair. Everything was going well. Nobody would think of looking for him here. The town must be buzzing with cops; but, once he'd joined the multitude flocking over Cabot Bridge to the stadium, he would become invisible.

And then the telephone rang. Chester went rigid. Ten to one, Sukie would mention his presence to whoever was calling. Or it could be somebody who *wanted* to know if he was with her.

"Will you answer it for me, Chester?" she called from the kitchen. "Tell them unless it's urgent I'll call back." He took up the receiver.

"Yes?" he croaked. . . . "She's busy right now. I'll give her the message."

"Who was it?" Sukie called.

"Girl called Emmeline. Wants to remind you about Sunday."

Sukie appeared, carrying a tray with a napkin, knife and glass. "Fuss-budget. Goodness, you're perspiring, Chester. Is it too hot for you in here? Though it really isn't. Are you sure you feel okay? I really don't think you're well enough to go to the game."

"Now, don't *you* fuss, Sukie." . . .

Nigel had gone out with Charles Reilly for an early lunch, thereby just missing the brouhaha set up by Chester's disappearance. Brady arrived at 12:20, seething with rage at the sergeant and his detachment who had let Chester slip through their fingers: the plainclothes man detailed to keep Chester penned in received a tongue-lashing he would not forget to the end of his days. Brady sent out the alarm to the city's police headquarters, and soon Cabot was swarming with cops. Every exit from Hawthorne House was blocked: everyone going in or out was asked if he had seen Chester Ahlberg any time this morning. But it was not till nearly 1 P.M. that the student Peter, hurrying in for lunch, told how he had met the tutor in the basement. Peter, questioned, described Chester's strange clothes and said he'd met him around midday.

So Chester had escaped the net. It was fairly certain he had got out through one of the side entrances to the House. Short-wave radio sets broadcast the news to all patrol cars. Nevertheless, Brady had the whole House searched from top to bottom to make sure, and himself, with the Master, had at once searched Chester's room which was quite unoccupied, and afforded no clues to its owner's disappearance.

"Anything missing, can you see?" Brady asked.

"No. I don't think so. Let me think for a moment though. Hm-m, why, yes: he used to keep a sort of stiletto—looked like a long, thin paperknife—at least he *used* to—on the desk here."

"He did? Jesus! We must warn his brother. Look, ring him for me quickly."

"You needn't worry about Mark. Nigel told him to leave town early this morning. He's gone to stay with a cousin in Gloucester, and only Nigel and I knew where he'd gone."

"Good. But still and all, I'm going to call the Gloucester police right now. Give me this cousin's name and address." . . .

Charles and Nigel left the restaurant at 1:50, and began walking toward Cabot Bridge and the stadium. From every side street people flocked in, thickening the main stream as it flowed more and more slowly toward the game.

"Hell of a lot of cops about," said Charles. "Wonder why."

A couple of minutes behind them, and unnoticed by them, out of one of the side turnings there emerged, in a press of people, a figure warmly clad against the weather: balaclava helmet, shabby tweed overcoat, a fraternity scarf (also picked up in Sukie's cupboard) swathing the neck and lower part of the face. Chester's purpose was formed like an icicle, pure, brittle, pointed. . . .

Past the sellers of programs and favors and peanuts, past the ticket touts, past the vigilant policemen at the outer gates, the vast concourse moved solidly, like a stream of treacle over the tough grass, then divided into several streams, each pouring through an entrance into the stadium. Nigel and Charles found their seats, high up on one of the concrete tiers, in a section behind the goalposts at the southern end of the field. Flags billowed out over the stands: the checkerboard lines over the empty field looked dazzling white in the sunshine, the grass from the distance seemed smooth as green velvet, artificial. Behind the sidelines, acrobats and cheerleaders entertained the crowd with wild antics, as if to release the electric tension gathering in the air. A band was playing, a perfervid supporter rent the air with spasmodic screams from a hunting horn.

"I don't see any drum majorettes," complained Nigel, raking the sidelines with his field glasses.

"This is Ivy League football. They keep sex separate from their serious activities."

"I like to see them prancing around, at televised games."

"Those huge bare thighs? Shame on you! And the Chocolate Soldier uniforms." Charles laughed. "They can't resist dressing up, over here. It's all part of the great American dream." . . .

A figure, its head wrapped in balaclava and scarf so that nothing showed but nose and eyes, slipped into its seat two sections away. Chester knew he wasn't near them but he knew just where Charles Reilly would be sitting: at the party in Chester's room, Charles had mentioned that he was going to ask Nigel to the game, and said his tickets were for one of the upper rows in J section. Chester congratulated himself on the excellent memory which had kept this piece of information in his brain. . . .

The wind struck bitter up there, swirling invisibly over the top of the stadium and stabbing downward. Nigel took out his hip flask, offered it to Charles, then took a nip of neat Scotch himself. The teams were out now—the blue of Yale, the gold of Cabot. They looked like miniature men, so far below—a child's idea of Martians, with their visored helmets and fantastically padded-out shoulders. On benches at the sides of the field the replacements sat, muffled up, glancing at their coaches who spoke to them with rhetorical gestures. On form, Yale had been the more resourceful team this fall, and the more successful: Cabot was streaky, showing flashes of unorthodox genius one day, wallowing in ineptitude another.

The officials, in their jockey caps and white pants, took up position. Silence came down like a huge hand over the stadium. Yale kicked off—a long, looping kick; the Yale ends streaked after it. The Cabot fullback caught an awkward ball over his left shoulder, avoided the right end with a feint, made ten yards and was submerged. A roar went up from the spectators. Yale formed a huddle, and very quickly the linesmen strung out, the ball was flipped to their quarterback, who danced five steps backward and sent a torpedo pass to a halfback who had run 'round his opposing end, but could only touch the ball with his fingers. If he had caught it, he would have been away. Yale was starting with a bang. But after a few minutes, the team had failed to make ten yards, and Cabot had possession. "Go go go!" yelled the Cabot men sitting all around Nigel. Their team soldiered on for fifteen yards, for ten, for another ten, before they failed to make it on a third down, and lost possession.

Thereafter, for Nigel, the game was a constantly shifting kaleidoscope, an alternation of storm and doldrum. Blue and gold linesmen colliding like wave and rock, with an impact the more titanic because from up here it was silent. The pauses when the referee and his assistant marched up with a tape measure, like field surveyors, to judge a doubtful carry. The light-foot dancing of the quarterbacks as they poised to throw a pass, their would-be tacklers blocked off to give them room. A huge halfback, hurling himself at the opposing line and leaping over a heap of prostrate bodies. The coaches biting their nails on the sidelines. Pauses while replacements streamed out onto the field, and other players trotted off. The bands in the interval performing complex maneuvers over the grass as they played. . . .

Chester Ahlberg looked at his watch. Less than five minutes to go. He rose, pushed his way to the end of his tier, walked up the aisle, then down the steps which led to an exit at the back of the stadium. It would all be a matter of timing—and of timing, as this morning had proved to him, he was a master. The objective was in his mind's eye, looming so large now that it blocked out the future beyond it. A continuous roaring, like that of a storm, came hollowly to his ears as he passed round the back of the stadium toward the entrance of section J. . . .

An hour earlier Lieutenant Brady had been at the telephone in the Master's rooms. He had telephoned every number on a sheet Zeke had given him, to inquire if any of Chester's friends or associates had seen him today. There were few replies: almost everyone must be at the football game. He had called, among the others, Sukie Tate. No reply.

He banged down the receiver in disgust and left the study. At the main gate he encountered a woman hurrying into the House.

"Miss Tate. I've been trying to get you. You wouldn't by any chance have seen Chester Ahlberg today?"

"Why, sure. He had lunch with me. You looking for him?"

"Is he there still?"

"No. He went to the football game."

Brady was dumfounded. A hunted murderer taking time off to watch a game of football. "Are you sure?"

"Well, he said he was going. He'd got a ticket. And he borrowed an old tweed overcoat of John's—said his own wasn't thick enough."

"Color?"

"Sort of browny. Faded. But I don't see—"

"Did he change any other clothes in your house?"

"No. And he left his hat behind. Went out without one. I thought it very foolish, with him just out of hospital—"

"Did he tell you where his seat was located?"

"No, Lieutenant. What are you—?"

But Brady was running toward a motorcycle policeman waiting at the sidewalk. "Our man may be in the university stadium. Brownish tweed overcoat. Alert them at the gates. Step on it!"

The cop kicked his engine to life and raced off. Brady got into the police car, where three bulky men awaited him. "Let's go." . . .

Two minutes to go. Cabot was two points behind, but on Yale's thirty-yard line. The vast crowd was possessed by delirium. Nigel swallowed the remains of his Scotch, and replaced the hip flask in the back pocket of his trousers. A third down. The ball was flipped to the Cabot quarterback. He darted diagonally left, and as he did so the big halfback ran behind him, making right. The quarterback somehow created the optical illusion that he still had the ball: he tore on, Nigel's eyes following him, and was felled by a blue shirt. Then Nigel saw that a movement was running out to the right. The ball had been slipped to the big halfback, who was almost away, with thirty yards to go. . . .

Chester Ahlberg, one black-gloved hand grasping the hilt of the stiletto in his pocket, stood at the top of J section aisle. He had picked out Nigel's tow-colored hair three tiers below him, in a seat next to the aisle. He gave a look at the field. His ears were closed to the crescendo of noise below him. He moved slowly down the steps which lay between him and his target. . . .

The big halfback, protected by his team's interference, strode on. He walked through one despairing tackle, and with a sudden acceleration, rounded the Yale fullback. Charles and Nigel, like every other Cabot man, leaped to their feet, to watch the halfback go sailing over the line. And, as he did so, Nigel felt something like the kick of a horse under his right kidney. He had jumped up at the very instant the stiletto drove at his back. Chester could not stop the blow: the stiletto struck, with maniac violence, the flask in Nigel's hip pocket, and was jarred out of Chester's hand.

Nigel whipped round, to see a figure leap up the steps, then disappear. The figure was unrecognizable, but he knew it must be Chester. He picked up the stiletto, fought his way to the exit and clattered down the steps. Outside, behind the stadium, he gazed left and right. His quarry had vanished. . . .

Running round the curve of the stadium, Chester climbed the stairs leading to his own section and emerged into the sunshine. Everyone was leaping down the tiers and flocking onto the field. In that multitude he must lose himself. He wanted to be obliterated, to disappear. The single-mindedness with which he had pursued his enemy turned into a pure impulse of escape. In the vast cheering, chattering, laughing, jostling crowd, he felt absolutely isolated: yet he had to hide himself in it, and sought out the thickest of the concourse where it pressed around the heroes of the game. He allowed himself to be carried hither and thither on the eddies of this crowd, twisting and buffeted like a straw in a torrent.

Chester had sloughed off the burden of the last few minutes— and weeks. For him they existed only as the rapidly fading memory of a dream. He was living in the present, in this milling crowd, his mind blinkered from everything except what lay directly ahead, his new destination. He must get out of here and go to New York, to his father, to the shelter of Abraham's bosom.

"Hi, Mr. Ahlberg. Didn't recognize you at first. Oh, boy, what a day!" It was two of his students, with their girls. "You waiting to line up for the march?"

"I guess so."

The little group was swirled away. Chester drew the muffler over his mouth again. He did not suppose the police would be looking for him here presently—not until that rat Strangeways could reach them to give the alarm. But there'd be cordons out; the bus stops, the railroad station, the airport would be watched by now. A state of panic went into him, like a hypodermic with some injection that paralyzed mind and limbs. He fought its influence. The first thing was to get out of the stadium. And his students had shown him how to do it. Chester edged his way, head down, to the far end of the field. . . .

The Cabot band was forming up. It was their custom, if victory had been won on the field, to lead a procession through the streets of the town, playing college songs. Any motorist who attempted to move through this demonstration would inevitably get jammed in it, for the rejoicing crowd filled the whole street from sidewalk to sidewalk, the effect of which was to cause traffic congestion all through the town. Some of the crowd was already streaming toward the four gates out of the stadium when the band leader threw up his staff, caught it, flourished it; the music and the march began. Both were, by tradition, disorderly—and got more so the farther they proceeded: costumes and hats were exchanged en route, for instance. So it occasioned no comment when Chester snatched a football helmet off a nearby head and crammed it on his own, the mouth guard concealing the lower half of his face.

There was some delay at the main gate; but the band, pushed forward by the mass of singing Cabot men behind it, thrust into the smaller crowd in front of them and drove them through the line of police outside the gate. Just before they reached it themselves, Chester snatched a trombone from the bandsman beside him, lowered the helmet's mouth guard, and applied his lips to the instrument.

"Hey, fella, that's mine!" said its grinning owner, and snatched it away; but not before the five policemen had been thrown back and they were out in the main road.

Groups of supporters caught up with the band, whose files were now sandwiched between them on either side. Behind them, thousands pressed on, making a 300-yard-long ram of which the band was the butting head.

"Cabot forever! Go go go!" sang the crowd. Trumpets and trombones blared: the big drum boomed, the kettledrums clattered: fifes and piccolos shrilled like a flock of starlings.

Under cover of the pandemonium, shuffling slowly ahead beside the band, Chester thought out his next move. He would follow along as far as the Square, just this side of the main university buildings. Then he would break away from the procession and dive into a taxi. The crowd would already have thinned out a bit: as soon as the taxi could move, he would tell the driver to take him to—to where, though? All the local terminals would be watched. Panic suddenly washed up against his defenses, in a rising tide. He'd have himself driven to Martha, a small town six miles away. There he'd hire a car from a garage proprietor he knew, and drive himself the thirty miles south to Manoosa, where there was a railroad depot and the main line to New York.

Chester sighed with relief. Once again he'd be stealing a march on Them. Tonight he'd be in New York, and dad wouldn't let Them do anything to him. A tear rolled down his cheek under the mouth guard. His neat little face—what could be seen of it, but nobody was looking at him—began to work, as it had when he was a child, fighting against tears. No, dad *will* protect me. I am his son. He'll understand why. He wouldn't allow Them to take my life away.

The main body was approaching Cabot Bridge, up a slight rise, and slowing down. At the intersection, motorists hooted angrily, held up by the stream of pedestrians. The head of the procession was faced by a row of policemen, spaced out across the near end of the bridge, and flowed past them slowly like a stream which must break up to run past a line of steppingstones. The cops were scrutinizing every person who passed through.

Chester was not tall enough to see them till he was only a few yards away. He stopped dead then, his eyes flickering to either side. But the crowd behind pushed him on remorselessly. Chester shut his eyes, allowing the sluggish tide to carry him forward: when he opened them again, he was past the line of police.

Now the sense of invulnerability possessed him again. They could not touch him—could not even see him, as though the helmet, the tweed overcoat, the black gloves had become a cloak of darkness. He turned his head to a student and his date who were walking beside him: he gave them a kindly smile, and the man winked back. They were now at the middle of the bridge. Ahead of them, the crowd was parting again, into two streams. Through the gap left in the middle of the road, Chester was soon able to see the obstruction.

A police car was drawn up just beyond the bridge, lengthways across the thoroughfare, leaving only the sidewalks to left and right available for the pedestrians. At one end of the car stood Lieutenant Brady, at the other end Nigel Strangeways, with a group of uniformed police between them.

Chester, as though an invisble force were crushing his heart, began to whimper. He could not understand how the blow he had given Nigel, though it felt as if it had struck bone, could have left him unharmed. "It's not fair," he whimpered, "not fair."

The gaily anarchic crowd had slowed to a halt before the police car. Each individual was allowed to filter past it only after a sharp scrutiny by Brady or Nigel. So much, Chester could see. He realized that his cloak of invisibility would be shredded away when his turn came to be inspected. For a few moments he stood there, frozen with despair. Then his nerve melted away, like an icicle in a furnace, and he suddenly turned, and ran crouching into the crowd behind him. Someone shouted. Brady looked up, glimpsing the back of a faded brown overcoat. "Stop that man!" he bawled. A loudspeaker on the police car took up the cry with a harsh, metallic bellow.

The crowd stood, clotted and bewildered, a vast herd of steers in a corral. They gazed curiously at the strange little figure which darted among them like a rabbit looking for a burrow. No one laid hands on it, but neither would anyone give way and leave a gap: they yielded only to the police who came shouldering their way toward the fugitive. Chester, moaning, felt as if he was try- ing to wade past immovable rocks through a sea of treacle. A hand fell on his shoulder. Desperate, he wriggled away from it, and found himself on the sidewalk, hemmed in, but he saw escape.

Nigel was one of the witnesses as the weird figure of Chester Ahlberg—in the tweed coat, the black gloves, the football helmet—scrambled onto the parapet of Cabot Bridge, shook off the hands that tried to stop it, and with a long crazed screaming hurled itself down to the river far below.

THE PERENNIAL LIBRARY MYSTERY SERIES

E. C. Bentley

TRENT'S LAST CASE
"One of the three best detective stories ever written." —Agatha Christie

TRENT'S OWN CASE
"I won't waste time saying that the plot is sound and the detection satisfying.
Trent has not altered a scrap and reappears with all his old humor and
charm." —Dorothy L. Sayers

Gavin Black

A DRAGON FOR CHRISTMAS
"Potent excitement!" —*New York Herald Tribune*

THE EYES AROUND ME
"I stayed up until all hours last night reading *The Eyes Around Me*, which is
something I do not do very often, but I was so intrigued by the ingeniousness
of Mr. Black's plotting and the witty way in which he spins his mystery. I can
only say that I enjoyed the book enormously." —F. van Wyck Mason

YOU WANT TO DIE, JOHNNY?
"Gavin Black doesn't just develop a pressure plot in suspense, he adds
uninfected wit, character, charm, and sharp knowledge of the Far East to
make rereading as keen as the first race-through." —*Book Week*

Nicholas Blake

THE BEAST MUST DIE
"It remains one more proof that in the hands of a really first-class writer the
detective novel can safely challenge comparison with any other variety of
fiction." —*The Manchester Guardian*

THE CORPSE IN THE SNOWMAN
"If there is a distinction between the novel and the detective story (which we
do not admit), then this book deserves a high place in both categories."
—*The New York Times*

THE DREADFUL HOLLOW
"Pace unhurried, characters excellent, reasoning solid."
—*San Francisco Chronicle*

END OF CHAPTER
"... admirably solid ... an adroit formal detective puzzle backed up by firm
characterization and a knowing picture of London publishing."
—*The New York Times*

HEAD OF A TRAVELER
"Another grade A detective story of the right old jigsaw persuasion."
—*New York Herald Tribune Book Review*

MINUTE FOR MURDER
"An outstanding mystery novel. Mr. Blake's writing is a delight in itself."
—*The New York Times*

THE MORNING AFTER DEATH
"One of Blake's best." —Rex Warner

A PENKNIFE IN MY HEART
"Style brilliant ... and suspenseful." —*San Francisco Chronicle*

A QUESTION OF PROOF
"The characters in this story are unusually well drawn, and the suspense is well sustained." —*The New York Times*

THE SAD VARIETY
"It is a stunner. I read it instead of eating, instead of sleeping."
—Dorothy Salisbury Davis

THE SMILER WITH THE KNIFE
"An extraordinarily well written and entertaining thriller."
—*Saturday Review of Literature*

THOU SHELL OF DEATH
"It has all the virtues of culture, intelligence and sensibility that the most exacting connoisseur could ask of detective fiction."
—*The Times* [London] *Literary Supplement*

THE WHISPER IN THE GLOOM
"One of the most entertaining suspense-pursuit novels in many seasons."
—*The New York Times*

THE WIDOW'S CRUISE
"A stirring suspense....The thrilling tale leaves nothing to be desired."
—*Springfield Republican*

THE WORM OF DEATH
"It [The Worm of Death] is one of Blake's very best—and his best is better than almost anyone's." —Louis Untermeyer

Edmund Crispin

BURIED FOR PLEASURE
"Absolute and unalloyed delight." —Anthony Boucher, *The New York Times*

Kenneth Fearing

THE BIG CLOCK

"It will be some time before chill-hungry clients meet again so rare a compound of irony, satire, and icy-fingered narrative. *The Big Clock* is ... a psychothriller you won't put down." —*Weekly Book Review*

Andrew Garve

A HERO FOR LEANDA

"One can trust Mr. Garve to put a fresh twist to any situation, and the ending is really a lovely surprise." —*The Manchester Guardian*

THE ASHES OF LODA

"Garve ... embellishes a fine fast adventure story with a more credible picture of the U.S.S.R. than is offered in most thrillers."

—*The New York Times Book Review*

THE CUCKOO LINE AFFAIR

" ... an agreeable and ingenious piece of work." —*The New Yorker*

THE FAR SANDS

"An impeccably devious thriller....The quality is well up to Mr. Garve's high standard of entertainment." —*The New Yorker*

MURDER THROUGH THE LOOKING GLASS

" ...refreshingly out-of-the-way and enjoyable...highly recommended to all comers." —*Saturday Review*

NO TEARS FOR HILDA

"It starts fine and finishes finer. I got behind on breathing watching Max get not only his man but his woman, too." —Rex Stout

THE RIDDLE OF SAMSON

"The story is an excellent one, the people are quite likable, and the writing is superior." —*Springfield Republican*

Michael Gilbert

BLOOD AND JUDGMENT

"Gilbert readers need scarcely be told that the characters all come alive at first sight, and that his surpassing talent for narration enhances any plot.... Don't miss." —*San Francisco Chronicle*

THE BODY OF A GIRL

"Does what a good mystery should do: open up into all kinds of ramifications, with untold menace behind the action. At the end, there is a bang-up climax, and it is a pleasure to see how skilfully Gilbert wraps everything up." —*The New York Times Book Review*

THE DANGER WITHIN
"Michael Gilbert has nicely combined some elements of the straight detective story with plenty of action, suspense, and adventure, to produce a superior thriller."
—Saturday Review

DEATH HAS DEEP ROOTS
"Trial scenes superb; prowl along Loire vivid chase stuff; funny in right places; a fine performance throughout."
—Saturday Review

FEAR TO TREAD
"Merits serious consideration as a work of art." *—The New York Times*

C. W. Grafton

BEYOND A REASONABLE DOUBT
"A very ingenious tale of murder ... a brilliant and gripping narrative."
—Jacques Barzun and Wendell Hertig Taylor

Cyril Hare

AN ENGLISH MURDER
"By a long shot, the best crime story I have read for a long time. Everything is traditional, but originality does not suffer. The setting is perfect. Full marks to Mr. Hare."
—Irish Press

UNTIMELY DEATH
"The English detective story at its quiet best, meticulously underplayed, rich in perceivings of the droll human animal and ready at the last with a neat surprise which has been there all the while had we but wits to see it."
—New York Herald Tribune Book Review

WHEN THE WIND BLOWS
"The best, unquestionably, of all the Hare stories, and a masterpiece by any standards." *—Jacques Barzun and Wendell Hertig Taylor,*
A Catalogue of Crime

WITH A BARE BODKIN
"One of the best detective stories published for a long time."
—The Spectator

James Hilton

WAS IT MURDER?
"The story is well planned and well written." *—The New York Times*

Francis Iles

BEFORE THE FACT

"Not many 'serious' novelists have produced character studies to compare with Iles's internally terrifying portrait of the murderer in *Before the Fact*, his masterpiece and a work truly deserving the appellation of unique and beyond price."
—Howard Haycraft

MALICE AFORETHOUGHT

"It is a long time since I have read anything so good as *Malice Aforethought*, with its cynical humour, acute criminology, plausible detail and rapid movement. It makes you hug yourself with pleasure."
—H. C. Harwood, *Saturday Review*

Lange Lewis

THE BIRTHDAY MURDER

"Almost perfect in its playlike purity and delightful prose."
—Jacques Barzun and Wendell Hertig Taylor

Arthur Maling

LUCKY DEVIL

"The plot unravels at a fast clip, the writing is breezy and Maling's approach is as fresh as today's stockmarket quotes." —*Louisville Courier Journal*

RIPOFF

"A swiftly paced story of today's big business is larded with intrigue as a Ralph Nader-type investigates an insurance scandal and is soon on the run from a hired gun and his brother....Engrossing and credible." —*Booklist*

SCHROEDER'S GAME

"As the title indicates, this Schroeder is up to something, and the unravelling of his game is a diverting and sufficiently blood-soaked entertainment."
—*The New Yorker*

Julian Symons

THE BELTING INHERITANCE

"A superb whodunit in the best tradition of the detective story."
—August Derleth, *Madison Capital Times*

BLAND BEGINNING

"Mr. Symons displays a deft storytelling skill, a quiet and literate wit, a nice feeling for character, and detectival ingenuity of a high order."
—Anthony Boucher, *The New York Times*